WICKED TIMES

An Ivy Morgan Mystery Book Three

LILY HARPER HART

HarperHart Publications

One

"I can't believe we're finally doing this."

Jack Harker glanced down at Ivy Morgan, the pink streaks in her dark hair glowing under the fading sunshine, and smiled. If he didn't know better he would think she was nervous. Since she was generally mouthy and opinionated, it was an interesting shift in her typically boisterous personality.

He reached over and snagged her hand, squeezing it gently as they moved down Bellaire's quiet street. This was their first official date. Sure, they'd already kissed so many times Jack thought his lips were going to catch fire, and they'd even slept cuddled up on the same couch for a few nights, but this was the real beginning. This was the big moment. This was the night that would change everything. Okay, if he was being internally truthful, maybe Ivy wasn't the only one suffering from a case of the nerves.

"Are you regretting agreeing to go out with me?" Jack asked, studying the soft planes of her face as she shifted to look at him.

"Why would you ask that?" Ivy was confused. "Did you change your mind?"

Jack sighed. He didn't blame her for being worried. He'd made it clear from the moment he moved to Shadow Lake – a small town in northern Lower Michigan – and taken up residence as one of the town's only full-time police officers that he wasn't interested in romance. That decree lasted until the first moment he saw Ivy. He fought her pull as long as he could, but finally he realized it would be easier to accept what he was feeling and give the relationship a chance rather than fight the inevitable. And that's how he felt. Falling for Ivy wasn't something he could run from because it was already happening. It *was* inevitable. Of course, she still worried that he was going to flee the moment things got difficult, so he was constantly nudging her away from that assumption

"I thought we talked about this, Ivy," Jack said, his voice calm. "I know you're ... nervous ... about giving this a shot. I'm terrified, to tell you the truth. That doesn't mean I've changed my mind. Quite frankly I'm more worried about you changing your mind now than anything else."

Ivy worried her bottom lip with her teeth as she mulled the words. "I don't want you to think that I don't want this, because I do," she said. "I just ... I'm pretty sure I don't want a broken heart and I think you're going to give me one if you're not sure that this is what you want."

Jack rolled his eyes. They'd been over this very thing five different times in a one-week period. Jack asked Ivy out to dinner in a neighboring town because Shadow Lake was small enough for their date to be considered evening news material. He wanted a chance to enjoy her company without everyone staring at them like they were trapped in a fishbowl. Since he issued the invitation, she'd called so many times to make sure the date was still on he wanted to shake her. One of the things he loved most about her was her self-confidence. She wasn't exuding any of that right now.

"Ivy, I want to start over," Jack said, changing tactics. "I want you to forget everything I said when I came to town about not wanting a relationship. That was crap."

"It wasn't crap," Ivy argued. "You were very adamant and you kept warning me to stay away from you ... even though I'd like to point out that you kept hanging around me."

Jack smirked. There she was. He loved that mouth ... in more ways than one. "I was adamant," he conceded. "You managed to completely throw me off, though. So, if you want clarification, now I'm saying that I don't want a relationship with anyone but you. Does that make you happy?"

Ivy wrinkled her nose, her expression adorable enough to flip Jack's heart. He had no idea how she managed to turn him into a mushy pile of goo every time he was around her, but he had a sneaking suspicion that was part of her magic.

"I don't want to start over," Ivy said, stubborn as usual. "You can't go back in time. You can only go forward."

Jack stilled in the middle of the sidewalk and fixed Ivy with a hard look. "Do you want to go forward with me?"

"Yes."

"Then stop complaining," Jack ordered, although his eyes twinkled. "You being so nervous makes me nervous and we're not going to have a good time if we're both freaking out. Don't you want to have a good time?"

"Well, since you actually made reservations at the only restaurant in town that serves vegetarian entrees … and you dressed up … and you smell really good … I guess it's fair to say that I want to have a good time," Ivy replied.

Jack smirked. "I smell really good?"

"Don't let it go to your head," Ivy warned. "Maybe you just smell really bad every other day of the week."

Jack took Ivy by surprised when he tugged on their joined hands and pulled her to him, their bodies forced together by the action. He ran his hand down the back of her head and rubbed his nose against her soft cheek. She smelled good, too … like peaches. "I don't think I believe you," he whispered, grinning when she involuntarily shivered. "I think you like how I smell every day of the week."

"I think you're full … ."

Ivy didn't get a chance to finish the sentence because Jack's soft lips covered her mouth. She returned the kiss, sighing into his mouth as he held her close for a moment. When they parted, her face was flushed.

"Why did you do that?" Ivy asked, her voice low.

"Because I didn't want it hanging over our heads all night," Jack answered. "We're both nervous. We're both … excited. I wanted to do that so we wouldn't worry about it all night. Don't you feel more relaxed?"

Ivy's sea-blue eyes widened. "Actually, now I'm thinking about you being naked."

Jack barked out a coarse laugh. She wasn't afraid of saying anything that came to her mind. He absolutely loved that about her. "I've been thinking about that since I met you," he said. "Why don't we start with dinner?"

Ivy graced him with a beautiful smile. "Then maybe we can go for a walk," she suggested. "I love downtown Bellaire and they have a great ice cream shop."

"You had me at ice cream, honey," Jack said. He knew that wasn't true, though. She'd had him since the moment their eyes locked.

"THIS IS A NICE PLACE," JACK SAID, SCANNING THE ROMANTIC restaurant before flipping the menu open. "Is everything here vegetarian?"

Ivy pursed her lips. Jack was a carnivore. It didn't especially bother her even though she didn't eat meat and considered herself adventurous when choosing food options. Still, she was trying to get a feeling about his preferences in case she wanted to cook a meal for the two of them in the future. "Do you like anything vegetarian?"

"I like you," Jack replied, causing Ivy's cheeks to burn when he shot her a seductive smile.

"You know what I mean," Ivy said, tamping down her raging hormones. "We really don't know that much about each other."

"That's not true at all," Jack replied. "While this is technically our first date, we've been hanging out in dreams for almost three weeks now. I think we know a lot about each other."

Ivy stilled. She was still getting a handle on the dream walking. She was a spiritual naturalist, taking a lot of her beliefs from the Wiccan faith and making up the rest as she went along. Her aunt Felicity was a full-blown witch, boasting the power to read auras and even cast the occasional spell when she felt like it. Ivy never thought about magic until she found herself visiting Jack's dreams.

They'd fought off his nightmares together – memories of being shot by his partner on a Detroit street haunting him – and then they'd proceeded to picnic, fish, and take walks in the woods. After an initial freakout regarding the shared dreams, Jack seemed fine with Ivy's presence in his head … mostly because Ivy informed him that he was the one calling to her without realizing he was doing it. Now he found joy in the dreams, and she couldn't help but share his enthusiasm despite her inner misgivings that he would grow to dislike them.

"I liked the dream you had last night," Ivy said, tracing her fork with a shaky finger. "I didn't know that Detroit had such beautiful scenery."

Jack snorted. "I don't think that most people who live in the city find the Detroit River beautiful," he said. "I wanted to show it to you, though. I spent a lot of time in that area when I lived down there."

"How come we couldn't fish? You usually want to fish because you claim it relaxes you."

"Because anything you pull out of the Detroit River is poisonous," Jack answered. "It would've literally killed you to eat it."

Ivy chuckled. "It was a dream. We wouldn't really have been eating it. You know that, right?"

Jack shrugged, nonplussed. "We're not really kissing in those dreams either and it still feels real to me."

Ivy pursed her lips. "You're trying to make me uncomfortable."

"No, I'm trying to get you hot and bothered," Jack shot back. "There's a difference." He was charming when he felt like it, and now was one of those times. "The last thing I want to do is make you uncomfortable. I don't think you're really uncomfortable, though. I think you're embarrassed because the dreams make you emotionally vulnerable. There's a difference."

Emotionally vulnerable? Ivy frowned. "I think you're as vulnerable in those dreams as I am."

"I think I'm more vulnerable in those dreams than you are," Jack countered. "I'm okay with that because … you never push me. You have a lot of different types of magic, Ivy. I think that's your neatest trick, though."

Ivy's heart clenched. "I ... ."

"Oh, wow, I've rendered you speechless," Jack teased. "That has to be a first."

Ivy struggled to collect herself. "I think you like pushing my buttons," she said. "You like to fight, don't you?"

"I like to fight with you," Jack clarified. "You get my heart racing when you fight. I have no idea how to explain it."

Ivy didn't know how to explain it either. He had the exact same effect on her, though. "You never answered my question," she said finally. "Do you like vegetarian food?"

"Well, so far you've only made me a few things and I've thought each and every one of them was delicious. I guess that means I like vegetarian food ... or maybe I just like the woman who made that food for me. Either way, I guess I like it."

Ivy smiled. She couldn't help herself. "You make me want to kiss you."

"Oh, honey, you're going to have to wait until we get our ice cream to do that," Jack said, leaning forward. "This isn't the type of establishment where you can make out with me. You're going to have to control your hormones."

Ivy's smile tipped upside down. "I'm going to show you my hormones. Just you wait and see what my hormones are going to do to you." It took Ivy a moment to realize what she said. "Wait ... that might've come out wrong."

"Oh, no," Jack said, his smile mischievous. "You can't take it back now. I'm looking forward to seeing your hormones. I think they're going to get along well with my hormones."

Ivy leaned back in her chair, flustered. He was the only man who could do this to her. "You're going to have to buy me a big ice cream cone for dessert if you want to see my hormones. You know that, right?"

"I'll buy you an ice cream truck if that's the case," Jack said. "For now, though, you're going to have to focus on your dinner and keep your hands to yourself."

Ivy slitted her eyes and lowered her voice. "I'm going to make you pay after dinner."

"I'm looking forward to it."

"**WELL,** THAT WAS A NEW EXPERIENCE," JACK SAID, HIS FINGERS linked with Ivy's as they strolled down the sidewalk two hours later. Night was upon them – a happy and flirtatious dinner in their rearview mirror – and yet Jack felt no inclination to end their date anytime soon. He was comfortable in Ivy's presence ... even when the mere touch of her skin sent his heart fluttering.

"You didn't have to get the eggplant just because I did," Ivy said, smiling at the memory of Jack's face as he sampled his entrée. "You put on a good act for what it's worth. I could tell right away you didn't like it and yet you ate every bit."

"I didn't dislike it," Jack clarified. "It was just ... different."

"Different good, or different bad?"

"I like things that are different," Jack said, affectionately tugging on a strand of Ivy's two-toned hair. "That should be obvious. If you want to know the truth, though, I probably wouldn't order eggplant again."

"I guess I'll take that off the menu options next time I cook for you."

"I didn't know you were planning on cooking for me," Jack said. "In that case, you can make whatever you want. You can be assured I will eat it and love it."

"I think you're just saying that because you know I'm not going to keep my hands to myself now that dinner is over," Ivy teased. She was feeling playful.

"I'm saying that because whatever you make tends to be delicious just because you made it," Jack replied, guileless. "Although, if you wanted to make steak and potatoes I can guarantee I'll like that."

Ivy snorted. "You're a meat and potatoes guy, aren't you?"

"I like to think I'm more than one thing," Jack said, pulling Ivy closer. "I do like a good steak, though." He lowered his lips to Ivy's again, taking his time and offering her a sweet kiss that was full of promise. His eyes were heavy-lidded and thoughtful when he finally pulled away. "Where is this ice cream place?"

"Huh?" Ivy was still lost in the kiss.

Jack snickered. "You've got a moony look on your face. I like it. I … ."

The sound of loud bangs filled the night, cutting him off. One … two … three shots rang out. Jack knew them for what they were without blinking an eye. He shoved Ivy in front of him, pressing her against the nearby building and instinctively sheltering her with his body.

It took Jack a moment to clear his head, memories of his own near-fatal shooting flooding his mind. After that things snapped into place quickly. The shots weren't being fired at the couple. In fact, they weren't even originating from their street. They were around the corner.

Jack took a tentative step back, allowing Ivy to face him, her features drawn and ashen.

"What … ?"

"Stay here, Ivy," Jack ordered, moving away from her.

"Was that gunshots?" Ivy was obviously confused.

"I have to go and check on that," Jack said. "I … stay here, Ivy. I'll be back for you. I promise."

With those words he disappeared around the corner, leaving Ivy alone with nothing but her fear to keep her company.

Two

I vy pressed her fingertips against the cold brick exterior of Bellaire's pizza parlor, silently counting the seconds since Jack left.

One. It probably wasn't gunshots.

Two. Jack only assumed it was gunshots because of his past … and nightmares.

Three. It was much more likely that kids were playing with fire-crackers than for someone to be shooting a gun in downtown Bellaire.

Four. Someone could be dead.

Five. Jack might be in trouble.

Ivy started moving without realizing what she was doing, quick-ening her pace as she rounded the corner. It took her a moment to focus, the limited light being thrown off by the nearby streetlights causing her to narrow her eyes to make out the scene. Jack was on his knees in the middle of the street, his back to her as he studied some-thing on the ground in front of him. An invisible icy hand squeezed Ivy's heart as she broke into a run.

"Jack!"

Jack swiveled quickly, surprised by her appearance. "Ivy, go back!"

Ivy shook her head, not stopping until she was next to Jack and could see why he was in the middle of the street. A young man was down on the ground, his eyes sightless as they faced the sky. He was wearing one of Bellaire's telltale police uniforms, the shirt darkening with blood from a chest wound. He was dead. Ivy was sure of that. Jack still applied pressure to the wound with one hand as he used the other to cradle the phone next to his ear and bark out orders.

"We need an ambulance here now," Jack bellowed. "Officer down!"

Ivy pushed Jack's hand away and replaced it with her own so he could relay the information to the 911 operator without distraction. She pushed down on the wound, knowing it was doing absolutely no good, and waited for Jack to get off the phone. After a few more tense orders Jack disconnected and leaned in closer.

"How is he?"

"He's gone," Ivy said quietly.

"He's just unconscious," Jack said, his voice cracking. "I ... ."

"It's okay, Jack," Ivy said, trying to sooth him as she kept her hands on the police officer's chest. "I've got him. I won't leave him."

Jack dejectedly sat on the ground and watched Ivy until police and emergency personnel arrived. There was nothing else he could do.

"SO YOU HEARD THE SHOTS AND RAN INTO DANGER?"

Tim Ellis was a Bellaire mainstay. Ivy knew him from their days as rival high school students, a brief flash of him celebrating on the football field flitting through her brain. He greeted her with a curious look – almost as if he was trying to place her – and then focused on Jack. The emergency responders buzzed around the fallen police officer, but they weren't showing any signs of urgency.

"I'm a police detective in Shadow Lake," Jack replied dully, rubbing the back of his neck as he focused his gaze anywhere but on the dead man in the street. "I heard the gunshots and ran around the corner to see if I could help."

"And you took a civilian?" Tim asked, arching an eyebrow in Ivy's direction.

Jack scowled. "No. I told her to stay around the corner where it was safe, but she never listens to a word I say."

Ivy narrowed her eyes. "Excuse me? I ran after you because I was worried."

"I told you to stay over there," Jack snapped. "You could've been … ." He didn't finish the sentence. They both knew what could've happened. Jack's expression softened. "Come here," he murmured, opening his arms so Ivy could step into his embrace. He rested his cheek against her forehead for a moment, purposely ignoring Tim's annoyed look. "I'm sorry you didn't get your ice cream."

"I think I'll manage," Ivy replied, squeezing his waist briefly and then releasing him.

Tim knit his eyebrows together as he looked Ivy up and down. "You look familiar," he said. "Where do I know you from?"

"I own the nursery in Shadow Lake," Ivy answered, internally rolling her eyes. He'd also hit on her at least eight separate times in high school, his ego getting the better of him despite how many times Ivy shot him down. Now probably wasn't the best time to bring that up, though. "You bought a bush for your mother two weeks ago."

Tim nodded and snapped his fingers. "You're Ivy Morgan," he said. "We graduated the same year from high school. Everyone in Bellaire used to drive to Shadow Lake because people said you were a witch and we were dying to see it."

Ivy frowned as Jack's shoulders stiffened.

"What does that have to do with anything?" Jack asked.

"Nothing," Tim said, shaking himself back to reality. "I'm sorry. This isn't the time. I just knew I recognized her and it was bugging me. If it's any consolation, she wasn't actually a witch. She was really hot in cutoff shorts, though."

Jack's face looked as if it had been carved out of granite. "She's still really hot in her cutoffs," he said. "I happen to prefer the skirts she wears, though. Do you want to tell me about your dead co-worker, or should we keep talking about Ivy's shorts? He's the one in the middle of the street."

Ivy rubbed her hand across Jack's lower back to soothe him.

"Where did you hear the shots from?" Tim asked, returning to business. "Do you think you can leave your date long enough to walk me through it?"

Jack was furious, but he managed to hold his temper in check. "That would be the highlight of my evening." He glanced down at Ivy. "Can you stay here alone for a few minutes?"

Ivy wordlessly nodded.

"Now, when I say 'stay here,' that doesn't mean follow me into danger," Jack pressed.

Ivy scorched Jack with a harsh look, which ironically made him feel better. "I'll be right back," he said, brushing his lips against her forehead. "Don't wander around in this area. Promise me."

"I promise."

Jack gave her another quick kiss to the forehead. "Let's get this over with," he said. "I don't like being so … exposed … after a shooting. Someone could still be out there … watching us."

Ivy scanned the trees on the other side of the street. She didn't sense any immediate danger. That didn't mean another kind of danger wasn't waiting for Jack down the road. That would be a worse form of danger. Ivy could feel it.

"**DO YOU** WANT TO COME INSIDE?"

Ivy shuffled nervously on her front porch two hours later, her worried eyes trained on Jack. He'd been mostly silent for their ride home, going through the motions as he hopped out of his truck to walk her to the front door.

"Not tonight," Jack said quietly, his fingers restlessly roaming the palm of Ivy's hand. "I'll take a rain check, though."

Ivy pursed her lips, a myriad of things on the tip of her tongue to say to him. She didn't say any of them. "Okay. Have a nice night." She turned to open her door, but Jack stopped her by pulling her close, hugging her from behind.

"I'm sorry this happened," he murmured, rubbing his cheek against hers. "I'm sorry I'm being so hard to talk to right now. I just …."

"It's okay, Jack," Ivy soothed, leaning into him and letting him tighten his grip. "This brought back horrible memories for you. I understand. I'm not angry. I promise."

"I know," Jack said, his voice barely a whisper. "You never push me. I don't want you to think I didn't have a good time. Up until … it happened … I was having the best time. I'm so … sorry."

"Jack, you didn't do this," Ivy chided. "We were in the wrong place at the wrong time. There was no way you could've known that."

"Next time we're going on a picnic where no one can find us," Jack said, kissing Ivy's cheek. "We'll be completely alone. I promise."

"That sounds nice," Ivy said, turning in his arms so she could rub her thumb against his cheek. "I don't want you to think I'm coming on to you, but are you sure you want to sleep alone? You can stay here … with me … if you want."

Jack arched an eyebrow.

"Purely platonic, of course," Ivy added, internally chastising herself. Did he think she wanted him to do something else? That wouldn't be good. Crap. He probably thought she was desperate and throwing herself at him.

"Of course," Jack said, chuckling lightly even though the senti-ment didn't make it all the way up to his eyes. "I would love to stay here with you – even if you torture me with platonic threats – but I don't think that's a good idea. I'll probably be restless. You won't get any sleep if I stay here."

"I'm not sure you should be alone."

Jack rested his forehead against Ivy's. "We both know I won't be alone when I finally fall asleep."

"**WHAT** TOOK YOU SO LONG?" IVY FORCED A SMILE AS SHE handed Jack a fruity drink – complete with brightly colored umbrella – and reclined in her lounger.

Jack glanced around the sunny beach locale, confused. "What are we doing here?"

"Well, I knew you were going to pick a dark space to flog yourself in – huh, that could go to a dirty place if I'm not careful – so I decided to pick a nicer spot for you to beat yourself … wow, my head really isn't in a good spot right now." Ivy's smile was rueful.

Jack smirked. He couldn't help himself. The police officer's death was eating away at him, and even though he knew this was a dream world Ivy concocted to drag him away from the real world, he couldn't help but be relieved that she took the destination choice away from him. He took the drink and settled in the open chair next to her. "I'm sorry I left you with dirty thoughts," he said, sipping the fruity concoction and making a face. "What is that?"

"Sex on the beach."

Jack pursed his lips. "You want me bad," he said, resting the drink on the ground next to him. "If it's any consolation. I regretted not staying the night with you – platonic or not – the second I left your place."

"I know."

She had absolutely no ego problems, and Jack found that refreshing. "Where are we?"

"I don't know," Ivy replied. "I just wanted a bright spot with a beach. I've never seen the ocean except for movies. It's probably from a movie."

"I guess I'm going to have to take you to the ocean one day, huh?" Jack asked, reaching out with his left hand to capture hers and bring it to rest against his chest. Whether he realized it or not, he was putting her hand over the exact spot where his own gunshot scars remained.

"I would love to see the ocean one day," Ivy said. "I've always dreamed of taking a cruise."

"Well, I'm not big on boats, but if you promise to wear a bikini, I could probably get behind that."

Ivy made a face. "Do I look like the type of woman who wears a bikini? I don't even own a bathing suit."

Jack was puzzled. "You can swim, though, right?"

Ivy nodded.

"If you don't own a bathing suit, how do you swim?"

Ivy shrugged, a mischievous smile playing at the corner of her lips. She was always bolder in their dreams. "There's a small lake about a mile away from my house," she said. "When it gets really hot, I usually wait until dark and then go skinny-dipping by myself."

Jack's heart rate increased at the thought. "Well, we're definitely doing that together."

Ivy snickered, enjoying their closeness for a moment before sobering. "Did Tim give you a name for the officer who died?"

"Mark Dalton."

Ivy racked her brain for a moment, coming up empty. "I don't know him."

"How do you know Tim? He's a real douche, by the way. If you're about to tell me you had a crush on him in high school I'm going to pretend you're not talking."

"I definitely didn't have a crush on him in high school," Ivy replied, rolling her eyes. "He asked me out a few times … and I told him no."

"That's my girl."

Ivy hated the pleasurable roll of her heart when Jack referred to her as "his girl" and forced herself to focus on something more important. "I'm sorry this happened to you, Jack. I can't imagine what you're going through right now. Seeing him on the pavement like that … it must have reminded you of what you went through."

Jack swallowed hard. "I froze for a second on the street," he admitted. "You could've been hurt because I forgot my training."

"Oh, get over yourself," Ivy muttered. "You didn't freeze. You threw me against the wall of the pizza shop and covered me with your own body. You were ready to sacrifice yourself to keep me safe."

"But … ."

Ivy cut him off. "I was there, too," she said. "You protected me at great risk to yourself. Don't think I didn't notice. I didn't appreciate it either. I can take care of myself."

Jack frowned. "Excuse me for living!"

Ivy tried to hide her smile, but ultimately lost the battle. "Next time we're shot at I'm going to throw myself on top of you and shield you with my body. How do you like that?"

Jack shrugged. "I didn't hear a word of that sentence after you admitted you were dying to throw yourself on top of me."

"You're such a pervert."

"Says the woman who keeps offering me sex on the beach."

They relaxed into the dream, their banter keeping things from getting too deep. It was the one thing Jack needed, so Ivy gave it to him without reservation. The real world could wait until morning.

Three

"You look a little tired this morning, daughter. Were you out playing with your new boyfriend last night? Do I need to have a talk with him regarding your beauty sleep?"

Michael Morgan didn't bother trying to hide his smile the next morning as Ivy greeted him at the nursery gate with a scowl.

"Ha, ha," Ivy said, rolling her eyes. "You leave Jack alone. He had a rough night."

"Oh, that's always what a father wants to hear before his morning coffee," Michael said, accepting the thermos Ivy shoved in his direction. "Did you two finally give in and embrace temptation?"

"Dad!"

Michael chuckled. He was used to his daughter's moods. She embarrassed easily – especially where he was concerned – and he enjoyed pushing the envelope. He liked to keep her on her toes. "I was just asking out of parental curiosity," Michael said, flipping the top off the thermos and inhaling the rich scent with an appreciative groan. "You make a mean cup of coffee."

"If you weren't my father, I would fire you," Ivy warned.

"If you weren't my daughter I would … ." Michael squeezed Ivy's cheek and gave it a good jiggle. "You're so cute. Other than the circles under your eyes, I would say whatever you and Jack did last night was good for you."

"I am not talking with you about that," Ivy said, wagging a finger for emphasis. "That's none of your business."

"It must've been good then."

Ivy inhaled heavily through her nose to calm herself. "If you must know, we had a lovely dinner in Bellaire," she said. "Then, as we were taking a walk for ice cream after, we heard shots. We found a policeman dead on the street."

Michael stilled, surprised. "I ... are you making that up to get back at me for prying into your personal business?"

Ivy shook her head.

"Oh, Ivy," Michael said, brushing his daughter's hair away from her face so he could take in her weary demeanor with a fresh set of eyes. "I'm so sorry. That must've put a real damper on your date."

"You could say that," Ivy replied dryly. "Jack was ... shaken up. We had to answer questions from the police for a few hours. As you can imagine, our night didn't exactly end on a romantic note."

"That must've been terrible for Jack," Michael mused. "After the way he was shot ... ." Michael broke off, realizing what he said when it was too late to haul the words back into his mouth.

Ivy slitted her eyes. "Who told you about that?"

"I ... ."

"It was Max, wasn't it?" Ivy charged. "I'm going to ... ." She broke off, miming strangling someone.

Despite the seriousness of the situation, Michael wanted to laugh at the display. He wisely thought better of it. "Your brother may have let what happened to Jack slip," he conceded. "We both know he has your best interests at heart, though. You might want to give him a pass on this one."

"Why would I possibly give him a pass?" Ivy was incensed. Her brother only knew about Jack's ordeal because the police officer bravely related the story to a local runaway trying to come back from her own tragic situation. "That was not Max's story to spread around."

"He didn't tell anyone but your mother and me," Michael said, his voice even as he tried to rein in Ivy's notorious temper. "He would never tell anyone else. He told us because we're family."

"He told you because he's a gossip," Ivy countered.

"That, too," Michael conceded. "Ivy, there was no harm in Max telling us what happened to Jack. We knew he went through something in Detroit, even if you were keeping it to yourself. No one is ever going to bring it up to him. I promise."

"They had better not," Ivy hissed. "If anyone makes Jack uncomfortable about that I'll ... . Max better sleep with one eye open. I'm not joking."

Michael wordlessly watched his daughter stalk away, pointed in the direction of the greenhouse, and internally cringed. Now probably wasn't the time to tell her that Max was on his way for a visit. That would be much better as a surprise – especially when he was fairly certain she was in the mood to kill the messenger.

"HEY, baby sister," Max said, poking his head into the greenhouse a half hour later, a leery expression on his face. "You look absolutely beautiful this morning. That pink in your skirt really sets off your ... hair."

Ivy scowled. "Max, I am not in the mood to see you right now," she said, viciously hacking away at a potato plant she was trying to split up and move to separate pots. "I'm going to do this to you if you bug me."

Max sighed. He loved his sister, but she was prone to dramatic fits. "I heard you had a rough night last night," he said, moving farther into the greenhouse but keeping some distance between his sister and himself. "I'm sorry that happened. I know you and Jack were looking forward to your first date."

Ivy made a face that would've been comical under different circumstances. "I am so mad at you!"

Max groaned. "Ivy, I didn't mean to blab Jack's secret to Mom and Dad," he said, plopping down on the floor and keeping his gaze locked on Ivy's small shovel in case she decided to use it as a weapon. "I kind of forgot they didn't know and I brought it up a few days ago. They were cool with it."

Ivy stilled, clutching the shovel tighter. "Why wouldn't they be cool with it? It's not Jack's fault his partner was doing terrible things and shot him and left him to die in the street."

"That's not what I meant," Max said hurriedly. "You know that's not what I meant. It's just … that's a lot of baggage for one man to carry around. He almost died."

"He didn't die, though," Ivy said, tugging on her limited patience. "You shouldn't have told anyone what he said. You promised you wouldn't."

"Hey! You're still my sister," Max argued. "I'm allowed to look out for you. I like Jack. I think he's a stand-up guy. On top of that I think he's about the only one who can put up with your attitude.

"That doesn't change the fact that you two are going to have to work together to move past that," he continued. "Jack is … scarred … from what happened. He needs time to work through it."

"Oh, well, I'm so glad that you know how to handle my relationship better than me," Ivy deadpanned. "What would I ever do without you?"

"You would cry without me," Max shot back. "I know you're upset about what happened last night, but … that's not my fault. I'm sorry I told Mom and Dad. That was your place. They were just … going on and on about how they thought you and Jack would be married by Christmas at the rate you were going. I wanted them to rein in their expectations."

Ivy was dumbfounded. "Married by Christmas? Are they crazy? We just started dating."

Max was relieved his sister's ire appeared to be shifting. "Anyone who has been in the same room with you and Jack knows that you two are so hot for each other that you're ready to start the bed on fire."

Ivy glared at him. "That doesn't mean we're getting married."

"I'm glad you at least admit you're hot for him," Max said, chuckling. "Before now you were denying it every chance you got. Now you two can be hot to trot out in the open."

"Max … you need to stay out of this," Ivy said, her voice petulant but yielding. "Jack watched someone die on the pavement last night. It was a cop. He can't help but liken that situation to his own. We're not going to be … starting the mattress on fire … anytime soon."

"Oh, I wouldn't be so sure of that," Max said. "Just because something horrible happened, that doesn't mean he's not ready to move forward."

"What if he's not?"

Max stilled. "What do you mean?"

"I'm so worried, Max," Ivy admitted, hacking at the potato plant again. "I just know he's going to break my heart."

Max sighed and reached for the shovel, wrestling it away from Ivy before she could kill the innocent plant. "There's no need to take it out on the potato plant," he chided. "It's okay to be worried. When you have feelings for someone, you can't help but fear the worst.

"The thing you have to realize is that Jack has those same feelings for you," he continued. "I know you don't want to see them because … well, you're you … but he does have them. He didn't want a relationship and yet he can't stay away from you. That's chemistry, in case you're wondering."

"Chemistry doesn't heal his wounds," Ivy challenged. "What if he changes his mind and decides he doesn't like me?"

"I wouldn't worry about that," Max said. "He knows he likes you. We've talked about it. He's giving up that fight. He wants you and he doesn't care who knows it. I would worry more about dreams tearing him apart. He's bound to have nightmares because of this."

"I can handle his dreams," Ivy muttered. "I redirected them to a beach last night."

Max ran his tongue over his teeth, conflicted. This wasn't the first time he'd heard about the dream walking, although he was still stymied by the mere idea of it. "Are you two really sharing dreams?"

"I … ." Ivy was caught. Talking about the dreams with Jack – the man sharing them with her – was one thing. Admitting to her brother that something magically wonky was happening was an entirely different story.

"You can tell me," Max prodded. "I won't tell anyone."

Ivy made an exasperated face.

"I really won't tell anyone this time," Max promised. "I'm just …
trying to understand. How are you guys sharing lucid dreams?"

"They're not entirely lucid," Ivy replied. "I mean … we know we're
in dreams when it's happening. We didn't realize we were sharing them
at first."

"What do you do in these dreams? If it's something dirty, don't tell
me. I'll be the one with nightmares if you do that."

Ivy reached over and pinched Max's knee. "You're so gross!"

"Ow!" Max jerked his leg out of Ivy's reach. "I'm going to wrestle
you down and rub your face in my armpit for old time's sake if you do
that again. I'm warning you."

Ivy groaned, pinching the bridge of her nose to ward off an
oncoming headache. "At first they were just … regular dreams. We
took walks in the woods. We looked up at the moon. It was so easy to
talk to him when I thought it wasn't really happening."

Max clucked sympathetically. "In other words you let your guard
down and him in when you thought it wasn't real," he surmised. "He
did the same thing. You two got to know each other for real when you
thought it was just your imagination running wild. Have you ever
considered there might be some design in that?"

Ivy knit her eyebrows together. "What do you mean?"

"Maybe you and Jack are destined to be together," Max suggested.
"Maybe your subconscious minds did what your awake ones couldn't
and brought you together."

"Maybe," Ivy conceded. "I'm not sure that's true, though. Jack
started calling me into his nightmares about the shooting. He relived it
over and over again. He didn't want me there."

"He might not have wanted you there, but he needed you there."

"But … ."

Max shook his head. "Jack needed you to help him work through
it and somehow you knew to go to him," he said. "That sounds a little
magical to me … like destiny."

"When did you become such a romantic?"

"When I saw you and Jack together," Max replied, unruffled. "I
saw a different sort of magic there. Why aren't you with him now?"

"I … why would I be with him now? He's at work."

"He's also struggling because seeing that cop dead on the street caused his worst memories to resurface," Max pointed out. "You might have chased the dreams away last night, but he's still living with uncertainty today."

"What are you saying?"

"I'm saying that … maybe you should follow your instincts and go to him instead of attacking that poor plant and me."

Ivy rolled her eyes, although something in her brother's words prodded her to realize he might have a point. "Do you really think he needs me?"

"I really think you two need each other," Max clarified. "Jack isn't the only one struggling right now. You've tied yourself up into knots because you're worried about him. Maybe seeing him in the light of day will help both of you."

"Hmm."

Max smiled as he pushed himself to his feet and dropped a quick kiss on the top of Ivy's head. "Tell Jack I said hi when you see him."

"I'm still going to kill you," Ivy threatened.

"My armpit is waiting with bated breath for your attempt."

Four

"What are you doing here?"

The words came out harsher than Jack intended, but seeing Ivy's beautiful face waiting for him when he left the Shadow Lake Police Station for lunch threw him for a loop.

Ivy scowled. "Well, hello to you, too."

Jack's expression softened. "Hello, honey." He moved closer to her, internally sighing as the sun glinted off the metallic pink accents of her skirt. When he first saw the ankle-length skirts she was prone to wearing, he felt like laughing. She had a certain Bohemian flare. Now he couldn't stop thinking about what was underneath them. "You look pretty today."

Ivy refused to relinquish her annoyance. "Are you insinuating I don't look pretty every day?"

Jack chuckled. "You look beautiful no matter what day it is," he conceded. "I'm sorry I didn't greet you with applause when I first saw you. I was just ... surprised."

Jack's expression was enough for Ivy to cede her agitation. "I'm the one who should be sorry. You're at work. I shouldn't have come down here. I just thought ... ."

Things were so much easier to express verbally in their dreams.

"I'm always happy to see you, Ivy," Jack prodded. "Did you come down here to have lunch with me? That would be a nice treat."

"Well … ." Ivy bit her lip. "I might have packed a picnic for us so we could have lunch just the two of us."

Jack stilled, surprised. "Really?"

"Oh, it was a stupid idea. Forget it." Ivy turned to leave, but Jack grabbed her arm and spun her back. "What?" Ivy was flustered.

"I know this whole dating thing is new for both of us, but I'm pretty sure it's not proper etiquette to show up at a man's place of business, offer him a picnic, and then take it back before he has a chance to answer."

"Fine," Ivy said, sighing dramatically. "Do you want to have a picnic with me?"

Jack smiled. It was the first real one he'd been able to muster all day. "That sounds like the best offer I've had since … forever."

Ivy's expression softened as her cheeks reddened. "I … ."

"You're beautiful every moment of every day, but when you're speechless you're exquisite," Jack teased, grabbing her hand. "Take me to this picnic."

"HAVE YOU FOUND ANYTHING OUT ABOUT LAST NIGHT?" Ivy asked, handing Jack a sandwich. There was no sense in beating around the bush. They were going to have to talk about what happened eventually. It was better to get it out in the open now.

Jack flipped open the bread and studied the meat between the slices, ignoring the question. "Is this real roast beef, or am I going to have to get my 'this is good' face ready for some fake vegetarian soy product?"

Ivy pursed her lips. "Why don't you taste it and tell me?"

"Oh, you're so cute I can't stand it," Jack said. "I still need to know before I bite into this. I might be allergic to whatever this is made of."

Ivy faltered. "Are you allergic to food?"

"It depends on whether this is horrible or not."

Ivy rolled her neck until it cracked. "It's real roast beef," she said. "I made a special trip to the deli to get it. I also bought fresh Swiss cheese, tomatoes, and lettuce. I was going to put onions on it, because I happen to like onions on a sandwich, but I didn't want to do that in case I decided to kiss you."

Jack smirked. "That was a good answer." He took a huge bite of the sandwich. "Good girl!"

"It seems I should've gone with my first instinct and put onions on it," Ivy muttered.

Jack grabbed her chin and pointed it in his direction so he could kiss her, taking Ivy by surprise. Instead of pulling away, though, she sank into it and only reluctantly separated from him when he dropped his hand.

"I'm impressed with your sandwich-making abilities, honey," Jack said, using a napkin to wipe the mustard from the side of his mouth. "I'm even more impressed because it must've killed you to buy meat. I'm sorry."

"I buy lunchmeat for Max every week," Ivy countered.

"Why?"

"Because he shows up at my house for at least three meals and if I don't I have to listen to him do half-hour diatribes about sprouts."

Jack chuckled. "That sounds about right," he said, poking through the basket. "What else is in here?"

"I made homemade potato salad with dill, chocolate chip cookies, and I bought a bag of potato chips because I don't know how to make those."

"You sure know the way to my heart," Jack said, reaching for the potato salad. "Not that I'm complaining – and I'm definitely not so don't turn this question into some big drama in your head – but what brought on the picnic?"

"Um ... the truth?"

"I would prefer you not lie to me."

"Max stopped by and we were talking and he ... um ... might've suggested that I was in a foul mood because I was worried you were in a foul mood," Ivy admitted. "He thought I would feel better if I saw you. I thought if I stopped by with a picnic it would be an excuse to see you without looking really pathetic. I think I might have failed on that front."

Jack chuckled. "You don't need an excuse to see me," he said. "You can come and see me whenever you want. In fact, I encourage it."

The tension squeezing Ivy's heart diminished. "Really?"

"Oh, I wish you weren't so worried about stuff like this," Jack grumbled. "Ivy, I want to spend time with you. I'm sorry about last night. That was not how I saw our date ending."

"I don't blame you for what happened last night, Jack," Ivy said. "Stop thinking that."

"I won't stop thinking that until you stop thinking that I don't want you bringing me food." Jack's grin was wolfish. "I happen to love food. You bringing it to me is an added bonus."

Despite herself, Ivy laughed. "We're quite the pair," she said. "I think we're both a little neurotic."

"We are," Jack agreed, squeezing her knee before turning his attention back to the potato salad. "You really went all out. Are there onions in the potato salad?"

Ivy nodded. "Sorry. I forgot about that."

"It's okay," Jack replied. "I just need to do this before I eat it." He slammed his mouth into hers again, taking her breath away with the kiss.

"Wow." Ivy checked to make sure her top was still on when Jack pulled away. "That was … I think I lost my sandwich."

Jack chuckled. "You can have some of mine if you're good."

They spent the next few minutes eating in amiable silence, Jack packing up their garbage and securing it in the picnic basket before patting the spot on the blanket between his legs. "Come sit with me."

Ivy glanced around. They were the only people in the park next to the police station, but it wasn't exactly a private location. "Aren't you worried people will talk?"

"Are you worried people will talk?"

"People always talk about me," Ivy replied. "I don't mind the gossip. I'm worried it will wear you down, though."

"Yes, you're quite the worrier," Jack said, reaching for Ivy and tugging her closer. He wrapped his arms around her slim waist after getting her settled and rested his chin on her shoulder. "I don't care what any of these people think about you, honey. I know who you are. I like who you are."

"You're only saying that now because you find me exotic," Ivy argued. "What happens when people start gossiping about you?"

"I don't know what town you've been living in, but Shadow Lake has been gossiping about me since I got here," Jack replied. "Everyone is desperate to know why I left Detroit to move here. Adding you to the mix merely makes me more exotic."

"Speaking of that … ." Ivy swallowed hard. "I found out today that Max told my mom and dad what happened to you. I'm so sorry. I … ."

"Shh."

"Did you just shush me?"

Jack chuckled, the warm sound vibrating against Ivy's back. "I figured Max would tell your parents," he said. "It's not really a secret. I'm not hiding what happened from everyone. I simply don't want to talk about it with anyone but you."

"Are you sure you're not mad?"

"I'm sure," Jack said, brushing his lips against Ivy's cheek. "Are you sure you're not crazy?"

"I might be crazy," Ivy conceded. "I had an absolute meltdown when my father told me that Max spilled the beans. Then I threatened Max with a tiny shovel."

Jack grinned. "What did Max do?"

"He told me he was going to rub my face in his armpit if I even considered going after him."

"Ah, it's good to see the classics survive every generation," Jack said. "Anyone with a sister is familiar with the armpit trick."

"Did you do that to your sister?"

"I did."

"Then you're a butthead, too."

Jack couldn't stop himself from laughing. "You're the one thing in this world that always makes me feel better. Do you know that?"

"I do now," Ivy said, lowering her voice. "I … thank you."

"That's a weird reaction, but I'll take it," Jack said, kissing her cheek again. "Go ahead and ask your question."

Ivy wrinkled her nose, puzzled. "What question?"

"You asked about Mark Dalton when we first sat down," Jack prodded. "I didn't answer because I wasn't ready. I'm ready now."

"Did you learn anything else today?"

"I called over there, but Officer Ellis doesn't seem keen on sharing information."

"He always was a tool," Ivy muttered. "Talk to Brian. He might know someone over there."

Brian Nixon was Jack's partner. He knew everyone in Shadow Lake – and his wife was the town's biggest gossip – but he was popular in neighboring communities, too.

"I'm not sure I want to do that," Jack admitted. "I'm thinking it might be better for me – better for us even – if I let it go."

Sympathy washed over Ivy. "I know you don't want to dwell on it because of what happened, but I think pretending we didn't witness this is going to eat you alive," she said. "Maybe if you keep up on the investigation you'll feel better when it's solved."

"That's … a weird way to look at it."

"Nothing is going to bring Mark Dalton back, just like nothing is going to change history and make it so you weren't shot," Ivy said, her pragmatic side taking over. "You might find … solace … in Mark's killer being caught. That might help you in ways you can't even fathom."

"You have a poetic soul, honey," Jack said, nuzzling Ivy's neck. "I need to think about it, though. I … you understand that, right?"

Ivy nodded. "You're a thinker," she said. "I'm a worrier and you're a thinker."

"You're also a doer," Jack pointed out. "You would've been on the phone with eight different people in the Bellaire Police Department until someone answered your questions. I made one call and then stewed about it for three hours."

"I think that's because you're a brooder."

"A brooder?" Jack cocked a challenging eyebrow. "What's a brooder?"

"You like to brood because you think it makes you sexy."

"Are you saying you think I'm sexy? I'm pretty sure I already knew that."

Ivy elbowed him playfully. "I'm saying that … you need to do this in your own time. I can't force you to do it in my time. It's okay to be wary and think things over. I like that about you. You don't jump into things without giving it a lot of thought."

"If you like that about me, why are you still worried I'm going to break your heart?"

Jack's question caught Ivy by surprise. "Because … for the first time in forever … someone actually has the power to break my heart."

"Honey, I'm going to do my absolute best to keep your heart – and the rest of you – intact," Jack said. "I would never purposely hurt you. Please tell me you know that."

"I do know that," Ivy said. "I just can't help but worry that you'll push me away in some lame-brained male attempt to protect me down the road."

This time Jack's laughter was almost raucous. "I'll try not to be lame-brained."

"Good."

Jack pressed his lips to Ivy's cheek once more for good measure and then sighed. "I don't want this to end, but I have to get back to work."

"I know. I do, too. I … do you want to come over for dinner?"

Jack's heart jumped. He had a feeling she was suggesting something else, or maybe that was merely wishful thinking. "I would love to have dinner with you."

"Do you have any special requests?"

"I'll eat whatever you serve, honey." Jack pushed Ivy to her feet, climbing to a standing position and lowering his mouth to hers for a proper kiss. "You make me feel better just by showing up. It's pretty impressive."

"You make me feel better, too."

Jack pressed another soft kiss to Ivy's lips before taking a step back. "Is it getting hot out here, or is it just me?"

"It's not just you," Ivy said, chuckling as she leaned over to gather the picnic basket. "In fact … ."

She didn't get a chance to finish what she was saying, the sound of a gunshot echoing through the park at the same moment severe pain slammed through her shoulder. The force of the bullet spun her, toppling her to the ground as Jack's anguished scream filled the air.

"Ivy!"

She didn't get a chance to answer before the blackness claimed her.

Five

Ivy woke up in the ambulance, the blaring siren causing her ears to ring as Jack clutched her hand and a paramedic worked on the opposite shoulder. Jack was ashen, his jaw clenched, and he looked as if he was going to pass out at any moment.

"What happened?" Ivy's voice was thick as she tried to make her muddled brain work.

"You're okay, honey," Jack said, his voice cracking. "You're … ." A tear slid down his cheek. "Oh, thank you for waking up."

Ivy was stunned by the show of emotion. Despite the pain raging through her shoulder, her only concern was for him. "Are you okay?"

Jack barked out a harsh laugh. "Other than having a heart attack, I'm fine. Don't worry about me. Focus on yourself."

Ivy shifted her attention to the paramedic working on her arm. She recognized him as Jimmy Douglas. He was one of Max's friends and graduated a few years ahead of her. "I'm not going to die, right?"

Jimmy smiled. "You're not going to die. It's just a flesh wound. It's going to hurt like a bitch for a few days, but you're going to be fine. You shouldn't even have any scarring."

Ivy turned back to Jack. "I'm fine. I'm going to worry about you now."

"Don't ... honey ... ." Jack struggled to collect himself. "Please don't do that. Focus on yourself. I ... I'm so sorry."

"Why are you sorry?" Ivy was confused. "You didn't shoot me, and I've given you plenty of reasons to take a shot since we met."

Jack pushed Ivy's hair away from her forehead with a shaky hand, his other hand tightening as he gripped hers. "It's going to be okay."

"I know it's going to be okay. You don't have to keep saying that. You're starting to freak me out."

"I won't let anything happen to you," Jack promised. "I ... I'm so sorry."

"**WHERE** IS SHE?" MAX HURRIED TO JACK'S SIDE THIRTY minutes later, the fatigued police officer taking a break from his incessant pacing to lean against the lobby wall.

"She's being treated," Jack replied dully. "They wouldn't let me go back with her because they said I was too much of a distraction. They forced me to stay out here. I ... she's going to be okay."

"What happened?"

"I don't know," Jack answered. "We were having a good time. She brought me a picnic. I ... she bent over to pick up the picnic basket and the next thing I knew she was spinning around. I didn't even hear the shot until it was already over."

Max studied Jack's wan face. "She's going to be okay, right? Jimmy said she was going to be fine when he called. I'm a little worried given your reaction."

"She's going to be ... fine." Jack almost choked on the words. "It's not a deep wound."

"Well, we'll never hear the end of it," Max said, going for levity. "She's a hypochondriac. You're going to have to get used to that. Whenever she gets a cold in the winter she acts as if the world is ending."

"This isn't a cold, Max," Jack said, his tone harsh. "She was ... shot."

"I know she was shot," Max retorted. "Don't you think I know that? I almost had eight different heart attacks while I was driving here.

I'm trying to make you feel better. I'm worried you're going to keel over."

Jack pressed the heel of his hand against his forehead. "I'm fine. Don't worry about me. Worry about your sister."

"Yes, well, my sister is going to be more worried about you than herself," Max countered. "Pull yourself together. She needs to see that you're okay."

Jack sucked in a steadying breath. "I'm sorry. I ... ."

"I know," Max said, lowering his voice. "It's going to be all right. Come on. Let's go and see Ivy."

"They said I couldn't go back there."

"And I said you could," Max said. "Come on. I promise it's going to be all right."

"THAT HURTS," IVY TURNED HER HEAD AWAY FROM DR. MARTIN Nesbitt and frowned as Max and Jack moved into the room. "Make him stop putting that needle in my arm. I don't like it."

Max smirked, dropping a quick kiss on Ivy's forehead before turning to the doctor. "I'm glad to see you survived getting shot only to freak out about a needle." He was secretly relieved to see her agitation.

"You know I don't like needles."

"That's why that whole 'I'm getting a tattoo' threat you bandied about senior year didn't scare anyone," Max said. "She's going to be okay, isn't she?"

Nesbitt nodded. "She's going to be fine," he said. "Well, she's going to be fine as long as she lets me treat this wound. I needed to numb the area before I can clean and sew it up. She's being a pain."

Ivy scowled. "I think I have the right to be a pain."

"You do," Nesbitt agreed. "I would prefer you not be in pain when you're inflicting it on others, though. I'm funny that way."

"It doesn't really hurt that much," Ivy said, her eyes drifting to Jack. He looked lost. "I'm fine, Jack."

Jack forced a smile onto his face when he realized she was looking at him. "I know, honey. You should let the doctor treat you the right way, though. You don't want that shoulder to get infected and have your arm fall off because you're being difficult."

"See, listen to Jack," Max chided. "You're going to be really hard to marry off if you're missing an arm. The attitude is enough to scare most men away."

Ivy narrowed her eyes. "I'm going to beat you when I get out of here."

"Not with one arm you're not."

Ivy let loose with a long-suffering sigh, resigned. "Fine. Poke and prod me. I just don't want to see it." She tilted her head and focused on Jack again. "I don't think I'm going to be able to make you dinner."

"Ivy ... ."

Max cut Jack off, worry the man was about to say something entirely stupid washing over him. "I'll order pizza for everyone," he said. "That's my idea of cooking anyway."

"That sounds good," Ivy said, her eyes wary as they searched Jack's face. He looked as if he was about to fall apart. She longed to offer him solace, but she had no idea how to do it. "Do you want to eat pizza with us?"

Jack frowned. "You were just shot," he hissed. "You can't be worrying about pizza. For crying out loud ... ."

Max grabbed Jack's arm and twisted it, scorching him with a harsh look. "Do you want to step out into the hallway with me?"

"Max, leave him alone," Ivy ordered. "He's just ... upset."

"I'm upset?" Jack's voice bordered on shrill. "You were shot. Why aren't you upset?"

"It's just a flesh wound, Jack," Ivy said, her face twisting. "I ... I'm sorry."

"Don't apologize to him," Max snapped. "He's being a ... butthead."

"Leave him alone, Max." Ivy's lower lip trembled. "You're making things worse."

"Don't cry, honey," Jack said, exhaling heavily through his nose as he tried to rein in his runaway emotions. "I'm sorry. I'm going to go out into the hallway and ... get a drink of water. It's going to be okay."

Ivy mutely nodded, but she looked miserable.

"Get your arm taken care of the proper way," Jack instructed. "Make sure you take care of that first and foremost."

Ivy nodded again.

Jack flashed her a weak smile, moving to leave the room and then turning back. He strode to Ivy's side and dropped a kiss on her forehead, lingering with both hands on either side of her face. "You're going to be okay," he whispered.

He left her with Max, trying to push the threatening tears in her eyes out of his mind as he trudged down the hallway. He moved toward the lobby, skirting to the side when he saw Michael and Luna Morgan hurry in the direction of their daughter's room. He watched them go, his heart rolling, and then he walked out of the hospital and didn't look back.

"I CAN'T BELIEVE THIS HAPPENED," LUNA SAID, FUSSING OVER Ivy as she tried to make her comfortable. "I ... this is beyond words."

"I'm fine, Mom," Ivy said, rolling her eyes as her mother attempted to fluff her pillows. "Stop that!"

Luna frowned. "When your daughter gets shot, you get to make a big deal out of it. Shut your mouth and let me handle this my way."

Ivy's irritated gaze bounced from her mother to her father. "Do you want to help me here?"

"No. Once your mother is done fretting it becomes my turn. I'm going to put her to shame." Michael was unruffled by the disgusted sound Ivy made in the back of her throat. "I'm going to double my efforts every time you make that noise."

"Why couldn't I be an orphan?" Ivy complained.

"That is not funny," Luna snapped, waving her finger in Ivy's face. "I've just about had it with you and that's a pretty impressive feat given the fact that you were just shot."

"I was barely shot, Mom," Ivy said. "It doesn't even hurt."

"That's because it's all numbed up," Max supplied. "It's going to hurt tomorrow. Trust me."

"That's why we're giving her painkillers," Nesbitt said, striding back into the room. "Okay. I checked over your X-rays ... ."

"Why did she need X-rays?" Luna interrupted. "I thought it was just a flesh wound."

"Mom, let it go," Ivy interjected. "I don't care what documentary you saw on Oprah's television network. One X-ray is not going to give me cancer."

Nesbitt nodded knowingly. "I see where this is going. Ivy is correct. She's not going to get cancer from this. I promise."

"I still don't understand why she needed an X-ray if it's just a flesh wound," Luna pressed. "Are you lying to me? Is this an elaborate cover-up to make me think she's not hurt as badly as she's really hurt? Oh, God, is she going to die? Tell me now."

"Okay, we need to cut down your caffeine intake," Michael said, cracking his neck as he pulled his wife away from the doctor. "You can see Ivy, right?"

Luna nodded.

"Does she look like she's dying?"

"No."

"Then she's not dying," Michael said, although he looked mildly troubled himself when he locked eyes with Nesbitt. "She's not, right?"

The doctor was used to Michael and Luna's eccentricities. Max broke quite a few bones during his athletic high school years – and Ivy broke a few herself – so he was accustomed to their histrionics. "She's fine," he said. "The bullet ripped through tissue in her shoulder. She was probably lucky that she was crouching at an odd angle when whoever it was fired at her. I've sewn up the wound and she's going to be absolutely fine."

"I want a second opinion," Luna said.

"Ignore her," Ivy hissed. "When can I get out of here?"

"You can go home tonight as long as you promise to be careful and rest," Nesbitt said. "In fact, I would recommend getting some dinner into you and then taking the painkillers so you can sleep for a good ten hours.

"Your brother is right, even with the painkillers you're going to be sore tomorrow," he continued. "You are not to lift anything at that nursery. You are to keep the wound free and clear of dirt. I also think you should probably have someone stay out at the house with you to make sure you don't overextend yourself."

"I'll be doing that," Luna said.

"You will not," Ivy shot back.

"I'll do it," Max said. "I'm used to her being a hypochondriac."

"I don't want you staying there either," Ivy said, grimacing when she attempted to cross her arms over her chest. "I don't want any of you staying with me."

"Ah, I get it," Max said, cocking a challenging eyebrow. "You want Detective Studmuffin to tend to your wound. That's what you're saying, isn't it? I don't think you're allowed to do *that* until your shoulder heals either."

Ivy, stilled, glancing around as realization finally settled in. "Where is Jack?"

Max shifted, confused. "I ... don't know. He's probably still out calming himself down. He's kind of a basket case. Do you want me to find him?"

Ivy shook her head, her heart twisting and causing more pain than the bullet. "No. I know where he's at."

"Where?"

"He ... left me."

Six

"Tell me what we have."

Brian Nixon jerked his head up at the sound of his partner's voice. "What are you doing here? Why aren't you at the hospital with Ivy?"

"Ivy is in good hands," Jack replied, his tone flat. "She's being taken care of there. I need to know what's going on here."

Brian sighed, exasperated. Jack was a pig-headed mule on a good day. Someone going after Ivy was not a good day in his partner's book. "We found the bullet on the ground next to the picnic basket. It's cute that you two decided to have a picnic, by the way. You're going to have all the busybodies in town atwitter because of that romantic gesture."

Jack ignored the dig. "What about the shooter? Did anyone see the shooter?"

"We're canvassing the neighborhood now," Brian replied, tugging on his limited patience. He understood Jack's concern. He wasn't sure how much mania he could put up with, though. "That park is open, but the shot could've come from any direction. What direction do you think it came from?"

Jack searched his memory. "It came from the east."

"That narrows it down," Brian said, shifting his attention back to his computer screen. "We're running the ballistics on the gun. It's not going to come back tonight, though. If we're lucky we'll have it first thing in the morning. If we're not lucky, it could take another day."

"There has to be something to do," Jack pressed.

"There is," Brian said, choosing his words carefully. "Ivy needs to be taken care of. She was the one who was shot. Your only job for the rest of the day and tonight is to take care of her.

"I called the hospital," he continued. "Jimmy said she was going to be fine and they were releasing her. Why aren't you there to see her home?"

"Because finding out who shot her is more important than listening to her and Max argue about pizza!"

Brian held up his hands to ward off Jack's imminent explosion. "You are a mess, son. You need to collect yourself. I suggest doing that before going back to Ivy. Take a walk or something."

"She was standing right next to me," Jack muttered. "She was right there and then … she almost wasn't."

"And I know what happened to you in Detroit," Brian said, lowering his voice. "This has to be hard for you. She's still the one who was shot. Pull yourself together and go to her. You'll feel better when you see her."

Jack wasn't so sure. "Fine. I'll leave. We'd better have those ballistics back first thing in the morning."

"Hopefully Ivy will be able to kiss that surly attitude of yours away before morning," Brian called to Jack's retreating back. He didn't get a response.

JACK DIDN'T RETURN TO THE HOSPITAL. EVEN AS GUILT ATE away at him for hours, he stayed away from Ivy's house. Instead he returned to his home, switched off his phone, and drank himself to sleep. He had to be sure he didn't dream. If she found him in his dreams, he would have no excuse. He couldn't bear the thought of those clear blue eyes accusing him of doing wrong when he already knew in his wounded heart that he was making a huge mistake.

Jack found himself in Ivy's favorite meadow when the dream claimed him, his heart rate increasing as he glanced around. There she was … sitting in her fairy ring. Her back was to him and she was resting her head against her knees as she sat on the ground and stared at the weathered tree that looked as if it had a wizened face carved into it.

Jack remained behind her, his heart clenching as he watched her. *Was she in pain? Did she eat dinner? Was she alone at the house? God, did she wait for him only to find he abandoned her?*

Jack didn't have answers to those questions. The ones he supplied via his imagination filled him with internal disgust. How could he leave her after she was shot? She was never going to forgive him. He didn't blame her.

Instead of approaching, instead of offering a lame excuse that would only hurt both of them, Jack settled on the ground and rested his head against the roughened bark of a nearby tree and watched her. He spent hours like that. He never uttered one word … and she never turned around.

"WAKE up," Brian ordered the next morning, tossing a glass of water on Jack's face and causing him to bolt upright.

"What the hell?" Jack sputtered.

"You were snoring loud enough to wake the dead," Brian said, moving away from Jack's bed. "What are you even doing here?"

"I … what … I live here! What are you doing here?"

"I'm looking for you because you were supposed to be at work an hour ago," Brian answered, his tone hostile. "Now, I wasn't initially worried because I figured you were at Ivy's house and you didn't want to wake her. Imagine my surprise when I found out that wasn't the case."

Jack stilled. "You didn't go over there, did you?"

"I did," Brian replied, irked. "I knocked on her door and found an incredibly angry Max on the other side. Don't worry, Ivy didn't wake up. They gave her powerful painkillers that knocked her out once she finally relented and let Max shove them down her throat."

"That's good," Jack murmured, rubbing his forehead. He had a killer hangover. "What did the doctor say?"

"The doctor said you're an ass."

Jack rolled his eyes and tossed the covers off of him as he shifted his legs to the side of the bed. His stomach felt queasy. "What did the doctor really say?"

"She's fine, Jack," Brian snapped. "She's going to have a rough day today, but then she should pretty much be back to normal. That is if she's done crying by then."

Jack rolled his neck, cracking it. "Why was she crying?"

"Why do you think?"

"I have no idea," Jack lied. "What did Max say?"

"What did Max say?" Brian was beside himself as he strode around Jack's bed and lifted his partner's cell phone. He wordlessly powered it up, his finger gliding over the screen until he found what he wanted. He put Max's voicemail on speaker so they both could hear it.

"Jack, I don't know what's going on, but Ivy is really upset," Max said, his voice calm. "She said you left her. I told her she was overreacting and that you were probably just out getting some air, but she's kind of ... hurt. Call me when you get this."

Jack's heart sank. "I ... ."

"We're not done," Brian said, waiting as another message kicked in.

"Okay, Jack, I'm not going to lie. I'm worried." Max's voice was cold this time. "It's been an hour. They're going to release Ivy in another hour. Why aren't you here? She says you're gone and you're not coming back. I ... don't you even think about doing this to her. This was exactly what she was afraid of. I ... call me."

"I'll talk to her," Jack said softly.

"Oh, there's another one," Brian said, his smile grim as Max's voice filled the air for a third time.

"I'm going to kill you," Max seethed. "Do you have any idea what you've done? You abandoned her after she was shot. You're a ... piece of crap. Don't you ever come near her again. It's two in the morning and she's refusing to take the painkillers because she doesn't want to see you in her dreams. She's afraid to sleep. She's in pain! I hate you. Don't you ever even think about looking at my sister again. I'm not joking. I will kill you."

Jack was gutted. Max would only say those things if he was at his wit's end. For that to happen, Ivy would have to be wrecked. "I … ."

"Don't bother making excuses," Brian warned. "I'm on Max's side on this one – which is why I'm deleting these messages so you can't have him arrested for threatening a police officer."

"I wouldn't do that," Jack said, forcing himself to his feet. "I … I needed some time to myself. I needed to think."

"No, you needed to drink and wallow in your misery," Brian corrected. "Do you know what I find interesting?"

"I don't really want to hear this."

Brian ignored him. "You were shot in the chest and left for dead," he said. "You then turned around and watched your girlfriend get shot and instead of giving her a shoulder to lean on, you abandoned her and made things worse. That's a pretty obnoxious personality defect you've got going on there."

"Is there something else you wanted to tell me?" Jack asked, shuffling toward the bathroom. "Do you have actual news or do you want to yell at me some more? If you're going to yell, you could at least make coffee while I'm in the shower."

Brian studied his partner for a moment. They'd only known each other for a short amount of time, but he could see the man crumbling in front of his eyes. Despite knowing Jack's tortured past, Brian was having trouble mustering any sympathy for a man who would do what Jack did.

He tossed the file he was carrying on Jack's bed. "Make your own coffee."

"What is that?" Jack asked, his eyes zeroing in on the file. "Is that the ballistics report?"

"It is," Brian replied.

"What does it say?"

"The gun used to shoot Ivy came up with two matches in the system," Brian replied coolly. "The first was a recent entry. Those results came in yesterday."

"It was Mark Dalton, wasn't it?" Jack was dumbfounded. "Whoever shot Mark drove over here to shoot Ivy. Why?"

"I can't be sure that Ivy was the target," Brian answered. "She wasn't the only one in the park yesterday. I collected her picnic basket, by the way. I was going to drop it off this morning, but Max's rage flustered me ... not that I blame the boy. He's always had a protective streak a mile wide where his sister is concerned."

"I don't care about the picnic basket," Jack seethed. "Screw the stupid picnic basket. Are you saying you think I was the target?" Jack swallowed, his mouth somehow dryer than it was moments before. "God. Are you saying Ivy was shot because of me?"

Despite his anger, Brian felt pity welling in his chest. The next round of answers would most assuredly be enough to drop his partner to his knees. He wasn't pulling punches, though.

"I told you there were two ballistics matches," Brian said. "Don't you want to know what the second one was?"

Jack waited, his patience wearing thin.

"The third shooting was in Detroit," Brian replied. "It was a little more than seven months ago."

Jack's heart hammered, blood rushing past his ears as he realized what he was about to hear. "No ... ."

"Yes," Brian countered. "The gun used to shoot Mark Dalton is the same gun that someone used to fire at Ivy yesterday. It's also the same gun your old partner used to plug you in the chest."

Jack's heart sank. "I ... that's not possible. Marcus Simmons is dead. He tried to outrun law enforcement when they were closing in on him after my shooting. He ran into a guardrail on the freeway and his car flipped over the edge and exploded."

"I'm not saying it's Marcus," Brian said. "I'm saying it was his gun. What you have to ask yourself is who had ties with Marcus. Someone managed to get his gun, and if I'm not mistaken, they're going after you for a reason. Why?"

"I don't know."

"You don't seem to know a lot of anything this morning," Brian said. "Why don't you think about it for an hour or so and get yourself together. I'll meet you back at the station in a little bit."

"What are you going to do?"

"Spend some time away from you," Brian replied. "You're not my favorite person right now and I can't drink to run away from my problems because I have a job to do. You need to take a shower, drink some coffee, and do some thinking.

"I'll apologize to Ivy."

"That's not what I'm talking about," Brian shot back. "You need to think about who is going after you. You've already fouled up Ivy's life. If I were you I would sear the memory of that picnic into your brain, because it's probably the last happy memory you're going to have with her."

"Don't say that," Jack protested.

"Son, I know you're hurting and part of me feels badly for you," Brian said. "That doesn't excuse what you did. You did the one thing you told her you wouldn't do."

"What?" Jack already knew the answer. He needed someone else to say it to make his misery complete.

"You broke her heart."

Seven

"Hey, kid. What do you want for breakfast?"

Ivy fixed Max with a dark look as she shuffled toward the kitchen table shortly before ten. "I'm not hungry."

"Pancakes it is."

"I said I wasn't hungry," Ivy barked, irritation with Max's jovial nature and her own hurt warring for supremacy in her muddled mind. "I don't want to eat."

"Well, you're going to eat," Max countered, refusing to coddle his morose sister. He loved her, but he'd often found tough love to be the best option when she got in a mood … and her current mood looked to be one for the ages. "I'll make you pancakes and you'll feel better."

"Did you ever think maybe I don't want to feel better, Max?" Ivy challenged. "Did you perhaps think I want to … do whatever I want for a change?"

Max ran his tongue over his teeth as he considered how to answer. "So, do you want blueberries in your pancakes?"

"Ugh!"

"Ivy, I know you're upset," Max said, his expression softening. "I know that Jack taking off hurts more than the gunshot wound. I can't tell you how sorry I am. I'm going to beat him up. Don't worry about that."

"Leave him alone, Max," Ivy said, her voice cracking. "Just ... let him go. That's what I'm going to do."

Max didn't believe her. "You're not letting him go. You're upset ... and you're angry ... and I'm hoping you're going to turn into one of those real housewives I see on television and beat his car with a baseball bat. You're not letting anything go right now. That's written all over your face."

"Let me be, Max." Ivy was petulant as she reached down to stroke her black cat behind his ear. Nicodemus slept with her the entire night, not moving as much as a whisker as she cried herself to sleep. He was the only thing she wanted to be around right now.

"I can't do that, Ivy. You're my sister and I love you."

The sound Ivy made was something akin to a wounded animal and Max couldn't stop himself from going to her. He knew that crying was the last thing she wanted to do, but he also knew that was the one thing she desperately needed to do. He pulled her in for a hug, holding her tightly against his chest as she dissolved into tears.

"I knew this was going to happen," she sobbed.

"I'm going to beat the piss out of him," Max promised, rubbing her back. "I'm so sorry."

IVY COULDN'T GO TO THE NURSERY – MOSTLY BECAUSE SHE didn't want to deal with the hundreds of questions she knew well-meaning customers would flood her with if they caught sight of her – so she opted to work in her own garden after breakfast in lieu of further wallowing.

Max put up a token fight, but when she promised to keep her arm bandaged and not do anything requiring brute strength, he left her with her beloved plants. She needed time alone to think.

Ivy was angry. There was no getting around it. Jack promised he would never purposely hurt her in one breath and walked away with the next. She expected it from the beginning. She had no idea why she was surprised. No, that wasn't true. She knew why she was surprised.

She believed his lies because she wanted them to be true. There could be no other explanation.

Ivy was so lost in thought she didn't hear Brian when he parked in the driveway, only looking up when he dropped the picnic basket close to her knees. For one brief moment hope flared in Ivy's heart, only to be cut short when she realized who was visiting.

"Thank you for bringing this back to me," she said, hoping her voice didn't sound as unnaturally squeaky to him as it did to her. "This is one of my favorites. I'm glad I didn't lose it." Along with everything else, she added silently.

Brian forced a tight smile. "How are you feeling?"

"I'm fine. It barely hurts." That was kind of true. The pain had diminished to a dull ache thanks to the painkillers. "They say I'll be back to my usual charming self tomorrow."

"That's good," Brian said, sitting on the bottom step of the porch so he could watch Ivy work. "How are … other things?"

Ivy sighed. She knew why Brian was the one making the rounds instead of his partner. "You can tell Jack there are no hard feelings," she said stiffly. "I expected him to walk away so I'm not surprised. I'm fine. He doesn't have to feel guilty."

"Listen, Ivy, I'm not making excuses for him," Brian supplied. "I just … he's got a lot going on right now. If it's any consolation, I think the absolute last thing he wanted to do was hurt you."

"That's not any consolation, Brian," Ivy replied. "I don't care, though. I knew it would happen – no matter what he said – and it's done now. I don't expect anything from him. If he's expecting me to make a scene … well … he's fresh out."

"I think both of you are in a lot of pain right now," Brian said. "I don't want to add to your troubles, but we got the ballistics back from your shooting yesterday. There are some things we have to talk about."

"Oh," Ivy said, realization dawning. "God, I'm so stupid. I thought Jack sent you here to make sure I was okay."

"No, he doesn't even know I'm here."

"Well, that's great," Ivy said, rolling her neck until it cracked and gripping her small rake so hard her knuckles whitened. "He didn't even care enough to see if I was okay. I … wow."

"Ivy, no," Brian said, immediately shaking his head. "You're following the exact wrong line of thinking. I do not want to get between the two of you – and I told him this morning that I was on your side – but he's killing himself with guilt over what happened."

"Of course he is," Ivy said. "He's a brooder. It's all about him."

"I know that's how it feels right now, but Jack is … a freaking mess," Brian said. "He drank himself to sleep last night and I woke him up with a glass of water to the face. He wasn't in much of a state to think about much of anything while I was over there."

"Well, that's the one good thing anyone has managed to tell me today."

Brian offered Ivy a wan smile. "Kid, I don't think you're grasping everything that's going on here," he said. "Jack cares about you a great deal."

"Yes, because you often leave someone in the hospital after they've been shot because you care." Ivy knew she sounded bitter and yet she couldn't seem to stop herself from piling on the vitriol. "I guess all those romance books I read as a teenager had it all wrong."

"Ivy, Jack is just as upset as you are right now," Brian supplied. "In fact – and I know this sounds awful because you were the one who was shot – but I think he's taking it worse than you. He blames himself."

"He should blame himself. He walked out of the hospital without even saying goodbye." Tears threatened to spill over. "He said he was getting some air."

"Yeah? Well, he found that air in the bottom of a bottle."

"Good. I hope he has a horrible hangover and throws up."

"We all hope that," Brian agreed. "I … ." He looked up when he heard the front door open, pressing his lips together as he regarded Max. "I'm not causing trouble. There's no reason to hover."

"It's fine, Max," Ivy said, waving him off. "We're just talking."

"That's good," Max said, jingling the keys in his hand. "I have to run out to the lumberyard. There was some sort of accident with one of the workers. I have to be there to fill out some paperwork."

"Is it anything serious?"

Max shook his head. "No. I still have to go out there. That's what happens when you're the boss."

"That's fine," Ivy said. "I'm fine. You can see I'm fine. Go and take care of your business. We've already spent more than enough time together for one twenty-four hour period."

Max smirked. "I know you love me no matter what you say," he said, tousling her hair. "I called Dad."

"Oh, Max! I don't need anyone smothering me today."

"He's not going to smother you, drama queen," Max countered. "I wanted him to know that I was leaving and you were on your own. I told him you promised not to do anything kooky. He's agreed to stay away and not check on you for a couple of hours if you agree to text him if you need something."

"Like what?"

"He's willing to beat up Jack, too."

Ivy scowled. "How many times do I have to tell you to stop saying things like that? You can't threaten a cop in front of another cop."

Max glanced at Brian, sheepish. "Yes, well, I already admitted I left a threatening message on Jack's cell phone last night, so it's not exactly a surprise to Brian that I'm going to beat him up."

"I deleted the messages this morning," Brian added. "I made Jack listen to them and then I erased the evidence."

"You're a good man," Max said, clapping Brian on the shoulder. "As a good man, I expect you to make sure my sister isn't crying when you leave."

"I'll do my best."

Brian and Ivy watched Max leave, raising their hands to wave before returning to their conversation.

"I'm honestly okay, Brian," Ivy said. "You don't have to watch me. I'm an adult. I knew what I was getting into when I let my guard down with Jack. I won't be making that mistake again. There's nothing to worry about."

Brian's heart rolled. Ivy was one of the prettiest girls in town, but she closed herself off because people judged her because of her Bohemian lifestyle. Jack was the first man to pique her interest in years. If she shut down now . . . . "Ivy, I'm not telling you what to do, but you might not want to write Jack off just yet," Brian said. "He still might pull himself together. Sure, it's not going to happen right away because of what we found out, but ... I still think it's going to happen."

"Well, I hope it works out for him and anyone he finds down the road," Ivy said stubbornly. "I ... wait, what did you find out?"

Brian explained about the ballistics report, going into minute detail so Ivy understood the ramifications. When he was done, she was flabbergasted.

"I don't understand."

"I don't understand either," Brian said. "Whoever is doing this has a grudge against Jack. He's the common denominator right now. It's not you. I ... he's crushed because you were shot instead of him."

"Oh, well, great," Ivy said, hopping to her feet and kicking one of the paver bricks that sectioned off her garden from encroaching weeds. "He dumps me in the dirt and still manages to be the wounded party."

Brian clucked sympathetically. "He *is* wounded. You are, too. Just ... give it some time before you completely cut ties with him. He's going to be a bear for the next twenty-four hours. Then I think he's going to fall apart due to losing you."

"It's too late."

Brian recognized the obstinate tilt of her chin, and yet he still had his doubts. "I don't think it's too late. You're entitled to your anger, though. Just be careful. If someone is going after Jack, you're going to look like an attractive way to hurt him."

"That's not true. If that were the case he'd be here to protect me. I don't see him. I don't think I'm going to be seeing him anytime soon. Thank you for telling me, though. I'll be extra careful until this is settled."

"You do that."

TWO HOURS LATER IVY'S FRUSTRATION WAS STILL MOUNTING and she had no idea why. She'd decided to push all thoughts of Jack out of her mind – just like he'd pushed all thoughts of her out of his head when he walked out of her life – and yet all she could do was dwell on what Brian told her.

This had to be killing Jack. She wasn't going to kid herself into believing any of his pain was because of her, but the rest of it had to be plaguing his soul.

Ivy lifted her head when she felt … something. She couldn't put a name to it, but if she didn't know better she would swear someone was watching her. She shifted, studying the tree line in three directions, and found nothing.

She shook her head and tried to return to her work, but after a few minutes she realized it was impossible. She couldn't get Jack out of her head and she was done gardening for the day.

Instead of going back inside, Ivy dropped her gardening gloves on the front porch and moved around her tiny cottage. It was her childhood home, her parents selling it to her so she could be close to the nursery when she opened it, and it was her favorite place on earth. She would find no solace in there today, though. No, if she wanted mental respite she had to find it someplace else.

Ivy headed into the woods behind her home, pointing herself in the opposite direction of the nursery and trudging into the heavy foliage. Normally she would go to her fairy ring when she was upset. That was the first place anyone would look for her, though. Today she was going someplace else. Today she was going to wallow in a place where she knew she wouldn't be interrupted. Today she was going to find peace if it killed her.

Now she just had to figure out how to do it.

Eight

Ivy picked her way through the dense underbrush, being careful to stop and listen to the woods around her a few times to make sure no one was following her. She couldn't shake the feeling that someone was out there – although she didn't feel like she was in danger.

She'd been visiting Duskin Lake for as long as she could remember. In truth, the body of water was barely a lake. It was more of a glorified pond than anything else. Still, Ivy didn't want to be bothered. She wanted a place where she could feel sorry for herself that was away from prying eyes – and more importantly, pity.

In truth, Max would be able to find Ivy at the lake when he checked her fairy ring and found it empty. Ivy wasn't worried about upsetting anyone else. She needed space from her well-meaning family. She needed time alone to … cry.

Ivy hated admitting it to herself, but that was what she really wanted to do. She felt like the world's biggest pathetic mess when she started sobbing the previous evening – and again this morning – and while she knew Max didn't hold either crying jag against her, she couldn't help feeling ashamed for falling apart.

She was Ivy Morgan, after all. She built a reputation on being strong and needing no one. So why did Jack's abandonment – something she told herself he was going to do from the beginning – hurt so much?

Ivy was so lost in thought she didn't initially notice the quiet figure sitting on a fallen log next to the lake. When he shifted, the familiar muscular frame tensing at the sight of her, Ivy's heart fell.

"What the hell are you doing here?"

Jack frowned. "What are you doing here?" He pushed himself to his feet, running a hand through his dark hair as he regarded her with red-rimmed eyes. "You should be in bed."

Ivy rolled her eyes. "You're unbelievable."

Jack's expression softened, although he was wary. "I'm sorry for leaving the hospital the way I did yesterday. I ... ."

"It doesn't matter." Ivy cut him off. She didn't want to hear lame excuses about how he had a job to do and that came first. She didn't want to hear how he'd changed his mind. "I knew it would happen. It's ... exactly what I expected."

"Don't say that," Jack said, his voice soft. "Please don't say that."

"What do you want me to say, Jack?" Ivy rested her hands on her hips and fixed her icy blue eyes on him. Jack already missed the hint of warmth and flirtatious energy he usually found there. "You kissed me on the forehead and said you were going to get some air. That was the last time I saw you. You walked out of the hospital and out of my life. I get it. Just ... whatever."

Ivy's eyes filled with tears and she hated herself for it. She loathed showing weakness, and that was exactly what she was doing.

"Ivy ... ." Jack was miserable.

"What are you even doing out here?" Ivy asked, impatiently brushing away a falling tear. "Why would you come out here?"

"You mentioned there was a lake behind your house," Jack explained. "I needed a place to think where no one else would be hanging around. I ... some stuff has happened ... and I like being by water. It helps me clear my mind."

"There are three other lakes within driving distance," Ivy snapped. "Pick one of those places to ... clear your mind. This is my lake."

"Why are you out here?" Jack prodded. "You should be resting. I … you shouldn't be wandering around after you were … hurt."

"Oh, you mean after I was shot?" Ivy relished the quick flicker of pain on Jack's face when she said the words. "Well, as you may or may not know – I'm going with the assumption that you don't know since you walked out of the hospital without even saying goodbye – I'm actually fine," she said. "I don't need a babysitter."

"I didn't say you needed a babysitter. I … ."

"Aren't you supposed to be at work? Aren't you supposed to be keeping the good people of Shadow Lake safe from the bad guys? Aren't you supposed to be doing the one thing you claimed you came to this town to do?"

Jack exhaled heavily. She was so angry he could practically feel it wafting off of her from ten feet away. He welcomed the anger and he basked in the hatred. He deserved it. What he didn't want to see was the underlying current of emotional pain that was fueling that anger.

"Honey, I'm so sorry," Jack said, fighting his own batch of tears.

"Don't call me that," Ivy hissed. "Don't … ever … ."

"I'm sorry," Jack repeated, holding up his hands. "I didn't mean to hurt you this way."

"I'm sure you didn't," Ivy said, another tear cascading down her cheek. "I'm sure you had the best of intentions. You didn't mean to throw me away. I get it. Just … let it go and leave my lake."

Jack took a step toward her, hating the way she shrank away from him. "I can't just leave you out here," he said. "We need to have a talk."

"I don't want to talk about it! I don't want to listen to you rationalize why you had to do this. I get it!"

Jack licked his lips, tugging on his fleeing patience. She was stubborn. It drove him crazy. It made his blood pressure spike and his anger flare. He could not yell at a woman with a gunshot wound, though. Even he drew the line at that. "You don't get anything," he said, choosing his words carefully. "You're just saying what you want to say right now.

"I know I deserve it," he continued. "I know what I did was …

unforgivable. That doesn't change the fact that we have to talk about a few things."

"No."

Jack pursed his lips to keep himself from saying something hateful.

"I don't want to talk to you," Ivy said, her eyes completely dry for the first time in a full day. "I don't want to listen to an apology. I don't want to hear cop talk about the shooting. I don't want to ... know you."

"You don't mean that."

"Oh, I mean it," Ivy seethed. "I can't even stand the sight of you. I wish I'd never met you."

Jack stalked toward her, ignoring the distressed look on her face as he closed the distance. "I'm not playing this game with you," he argued. "We're going to talk and ... well ... you're going to shut up and listen to what I have to say." He reached for her shoulders, realizing at the last second that he couldn't hold her in place that way because of her wound and shifting his hands so they grabbed onto her hips. "Now ... ."

Ivy lashed out, smacking him across the face as hard as she could and taking him by surprise. "Don't touch me!"

Jack released her hips and rubbed his chin, impressed with the force she managed to put behind the slap until he saw her grimace of pain. She'd used her injured shoulder to give the slap some oomph. "Are you okay?"

"I just slapped you," Ivy replied. "I ... how can you even ask me if I'm okay?"

"Because I deserved to be slapped."

"You deserve to be run over by a car and then backed over again," Ivy countered. "You're lucky I don't have a vehicle with me."

Jack fought the urge to smile, knowing it was the exact worst thing he could do, but the situation was so surreal he couldn't fight the expression. Twenty-four hours earlier they were having the time of their lives on a picnic blanket. He could touch her without reservation. Now she was right in front of him and yet she still felt miles away.

"This is not funny!" Ivy went to place her hands on her hips and groaned, instead reaching for her bad shoulder. "Are you happy? Now my arm really is going to fall off."

Jack sobered. "I'm not happy. I don't think I've ever been this unhappy."

"Whatever," Ivy said, rolling her eyes and refusing to fall for his act. "You know what? You can have the lake. I'm going home." She turned and flounced back in the opposite direction, her hand resting protectively over her shoulder.

Jack immediately fell into step behind her, keeping two feet between them, but refusing to let her wander off on her own.

Ivy ignored the sound of his footsteps for as long as she could, but after a few minutes she swiveled and fixed him with a murderous look. "Why are you following me?"

"Because we have to talk." It was easier for Jack to keep his temper in check this time. Her pain put everything in perspective. "I'm going to walk you back to your house, check your shoulder, tell you what I have to tell you and then … ." And then what? Would he really be able to walk away again?

"And then you'll go," Ivy finished for him. "Great. This sounds exactly how I wanted to spend my afternoon. I think I must be the luckiest woman in the world."

Jack didn't know about lucky – although that bullet might have killed her if she hadn't bent over exactly when she did – but he was convinced she was the most beautiful woman in the world.

"Start moving, Ivy," Jack said quietly. "It looks like it's going to storm."

"Oh, bite me."

"WHAT DID THE DOCTOR SAY ABOUT GIVING YOU PAIN KILLERS?" Jack asked, his fingers gentle as they prodded the bandage over her wound as she sat in a kitchen chair and allowed him to tend her wound. "Hold still while I take this off. I don't want to hurt you."

After the longest twenty-minute hike of his life, Jack followed Ivy into her cottage – despite the fact that she tried to shut the door in his face – and patiently set about checking her shoulder. He was done yelling at her. Well, at least for now.

"You've already hurt me." Ivy was petulant.

"I know I have," Jack said softly. "You'll never know how sorry I am for causing you one moment of pain."

"Then why did you do it?"

"I ... panicked."

Ivy stilled, her expression thoughtful as she studied his intent face. He didn't meet her gaze, afraid he would fall into those eyes and never find his way back out. Instead, he pulled the bandage off and frowned at the angry wound.

In the grand scheme of things, it wasn't a bad wound. It was nothing compared to the mess left on his chest after Marcus shot him. The sight of the marred and angry flesh caused his heart to constrict all the same. This was his fault.

"Everyone panics, Jack," Ivy said. "It's what you do after that's important."

"And I let you down."

"I think you let yourself down," Ivy replied. "Just slap a new bandage on that and say what you have to say."

Jack licked his lips. "I'm the reason you were shot." It took everything he had to admit it, and he waited for her to slap him again before risking a look at her annoyed face. "It's my fault."

"You're just ... an idiot!"

Jack was taken aback. "Excuse me?"

"It's not your fault, Jack. You didn't shoot me."

"The gun used to kill Mark Dalton ... the gun used to shoot you ... is my old partner's weapon," Jack said, his voice wavering. "Someone went after you because of me."

"And you put yourself in danger to save me from Heath and Gil Thorpe," Ivy reminded him. "If you died in either of those instances, would that have been my fault?"

"Of course not. That's different."

"Why?"

"Because ... ." Jack was at a loss for how to answer.

"Because I'm a girl?" Ivy pressed. "Because you're a big, strong cop and I'm a weak girl? Is that it?"

"Oh, don't play that game," Jack snapped, affixing a new bandage to Ivy's shoulder and taping it in place as he tried to control his racing heart. "You're stronger than anyone I know. That was my job, though."

"Oh." Ivy's eyes flashed. "Are you saying you only did what you did because it was your job? And here I thought it was because you cared about me. I'm such a moron."

"I do care about you," Jack hissed. "You have no idea how much I care. I just ... I did this to you. Don't you understand that?"

"No," Ivy replied, fumbling with the top of her pain medication bottle and then popping two capsules into her mouth. She grabbed the half-empty bottle of water on the table and downed the medication under Jack's watchful eye. "You didn't do this to me, Jack. This was done to both of us. The difference is, I'm not the type of person to throw everything away because I'm afraid."

Ivy got to her feet and pushed past him. "I'm sure you know the way out."

"What are you doing?" Jack asked. "We're not done talking yet."

"Oh, yes we are," Ivy said, moving down the hallway and toward her bedroom. "Those were the pills that knock me out. I didn't sleep well last night. I'm exhausted. I ... hurt. I can't deal with you making excuses. I'm tired."

Jack frowned as he followed her, hating that he couldn't stop watching as she unsnapped her pants and let them fall to the floor, revealing a pair of black panties that caused his heart to speed up. "I ... ."

"Go and do what you want to do, Jack," Ivy mumbled, climbing under the covers. "Do what's right for you. You don't care about what's right for me. You've made that obvious."

"That is not true. Stop saying that." Jack was flustered. "I ... we're not done talking, Ivy. You're in danger."

"I'm done talking," Ivy said, her eyes heavy as she closed them. "I just want my heart to stop hurting."

Jack fought back tears at the words even as he worked to tamp down his irritation. He moved to Ivy's side. "We need to finish this conversation."

Ivy didn't answer, her breathing already steady as she slipped off into dreamland.

"Ivy?"

She didn't answer.

Jack didn't know what to do. He was nowhere near done talking to her. They had to come up with a plan to keep her safe until he could figure out who was after him. For lack of a better idea, Jack removed his shoes and climbed into bed next to her. His initial plan was to remain on top of the covers, but the second he felt her body turn in his direction he gave in to what his heart wanted and slid underneath them.

Ivy's body was warm as she rested her head against his shoulder, making a soft murmuring sound as she slumbered. Jack slipped his arm under her waist and pulled her against him, almost crying out because she felt so good in his arms.

"I'm only doing this because we still need to talk and I'm exhausted, too," Jack said, although he knew Ivy was beyond hearing him. "I'm not doing this for any other reason."

Even Jack didn't believe it. He smoothed her hair down and rested his cheek against her forehead. "You're killing me. I can't be responsible for killing you, though."

Jack held up a one-sided conversation for a few more minutes, but Ivy's mere presence was enough solace to relax him. Before he knew it, the storm raged outside as peace found him inside.

His last thought was of her anguished face before sleep claimed him.

Nine

Jack woke slowly, sleep trying to drag him back down even as he fought to get his bearings. Ivy's bedroom was mostly dark, only a thin sliver of light filtering in as the sun finished its descent into the horizon outside. He was in exactly the same spot as when he fell asleep, Ivy clutched against his chest.

She was still out, her face placid and angelic in sleep. He traced the line of her cheek as he watched her. He couldn't stand being away from her. He hated it. He'd hurt and disappointed her, and then the moment she was too weak to stop him he'd climbed into her bed so he could take comfort in her even though it was the last thing she wanted.

That didn't seem fair.

Jack knew she was going to be an unholy terror when she woke and found him holding her. That didn't stop him from doing it. Instead he spent the next twenty minutes running his finger over every inch of her face, touching her lips and smoothing her eyebrows. He wanted to memorize every inch of her, because he was pretty sure he'd never be this close to happiness again.

That thought was enough to fill Jack with insurmountable dread.

He'd only known her a few weeks and yet the thought of letting her go paralyzed him. How was he supposed to do this?

Suddenly Jack realized he couldn't do it. He couldn't look her in the eye and walk away. He wasn't capable of physically doing it. He would crumble, and if he crumbled and followed his heart her life would be in danger. He couldn't do that.

Jack pressed a soft kiss to Ivy's forehead. "You'll never know how sorry I am. I can't let you die, though." His voice was barely a whisper.

He was careful as he slipped his arm from beneath her, lowering her head to the pillow so she wouldn't stir. He tucked the blankets in close, slipping her feet – which always ended up peeking out from underneath the covers as she slept – back beneath the sheet.

He'd leave her a note. He told himself that was the best thing to do even as his heart fractured. He wouldn't leave without saying goodbye. Not again. She would break if he did anything of the sort, and he couldn't stand the thought of that.

He searched the end of the bed for his shoes, holding them in his hand as he studied her still silhouette. He would give anything in the world to crawl back in that bed with her and fix things. He knew that wasn't going to be an option. He kept telling himself that he would apologize when it was all said and done. He would win her back then. Deep down he knew it would never be the same because he'd already lost her trust.

Jack exhaled heavily and turned to the door, his fingers wrapping around the handle as his heart urged him to look at her one more time. Jack impulsively turned back to find Ivy sitting up in bed, her eyes glittering with unspoken accusation as they met his across the room.

"Oh, honey ... ."

IVY DIDN'T KNOW WHO SHE WAS MORE FURIOUS WITH, JACK OR herself. She woke from her heavy sleep – realizing she hadn't dreamed for the first time in weeks – to find Jack slinking out of her bedroom.

"Well, I guess I shouldn't be surprised."

"Ivy, I was going to leave a note on your counter," Jack offered, realizing how lame the explanation sounded before the words even finished leaving his mouth. "I didn't want to wake you up. You need your rest."

"Yes, and you don't want to deal with me," Ivy said, throwing the covers off her body and climbing out of bed.

Jack almost growled at the sight of those stupid panties again. She was trying to torture him. There could be no other explanation.

Instead of reclaiming her canvas trousers from the floor, Ivy yanked a pair of yoga pants out of the dresser and shimmied into them. By the time she reached the door she was completely put together – well, except for the adorable bedhead – and the look she sent Jack was chilling. "Are you just going to stand there, or do you need my help to open the door?"

"What?" Jack was still fixated on the memory of her pale skin before she covered herself.

"Can you only open the door when you're going to sneak out and abandon me, or can you do it with an audience, too?"

Jack snapped back to reality. Now was not the time to ... he couldn't help but wonder if her bra matched her panties. Wait, now definitely wasn't the time for that. "After you, Your Highness," Jack said, throwing open the door and bowing low so Ivy could stride into the hallway ahead of him.

Jack watched her hips swing as she walked, cursing himself for this entire mess, and frowning when he saw Ivy head straight for the refrigerator. "What are you doing?"

"What does it look like I'm doing?" Ivy shoved her hair away from her face and focused on the contents of her refrigerator.

"Ivy, I ... can't stay for dinner," Jack said, swallowing the lump in his throat. He was going to crush her all over again. He didn't have a choice, though. He missed an entire day of work – texting Brian that he would be in later in the afternoon – and now he had to make up the time. There was an enemy out there, and if he had any shot of making things right with Ivy – no matter how remote – he was going to have to solve this case first. "I'm really sorry. Any other time I would ... ."

Ivy knit her eyebrows together. "Did I miss the part of the conversation where I invited you to dinner?"

"I … ." Jack's cheeks burned as he realized how far he'd overreached. "I guess you didn't."

"No," Ivy agreed, turning back to the refrigerator. "I most certainly did not invite you to dinner. Do you know what's funny, though?" Ivy glanced back at him. "I was supposed to make you dinner last night. I thought we would finally get a chance to … ."

Jack knew what she thought they would finally get a chance to do. He'd indulged in the same daydream before she was shot. "Ivy, I am so … ."

"Don't say you're sorry again," Ivy ordered, shaking her finger. "Don't you dare say it!"

Under any other circumstances Jack would've found her righteous indignation comical. He would've gladly spent the next twenty minutes teasing her until she gave in and kissed him senseless. He could only hope that would be in their future again … somehow.

"We need to have a quick talk," Jack said, his voice low. "Whoever is after me might go after you again. You're important to me, which means if someone is trying to hurt me they'll go after you."

"Oh, that's such a crock of crap," Ivy shot back. "If I was in real danger you would be camped out on my couch to protect me … like last time. You're not worried about me. You're worried about me causing a scene and embarrassing you. Don't worry your pretty little head about it. I have no intention of even acknowledging you're alive from here on out. You are essentially dead to me."

Jack scowled. If she was trying to get under his skin she was doing a bang-up job of it. "You listen to me … ."

"No, I'm done listening to you," Ivy said, cutting him off. "You are not my boss and you're not my father. I'm my own boss and … well … technically I'm my father's boss, too. Although, he never listens to me no matter what I say. I guess you two have that in common."

"Ivy, I don't care how angry you are with me, you're damned well going to listen to me," Jack growled. "I have been to hell and back again and the only thing I know with absolute certainty is that I cannot let anything happen to you.

"I barely made it off the operating table and I had months of physical therapy before I was on my feet," he continued. "Putting you at arm's length hurts ten times more than that ever did."

Ivy narrowed her eyes. "Liar."

"Oh, stuff it," Jack snapped, taking both of them by surprise.

"Don't tell me what to do!"

"Shut your mouth."

"You shut your mouth!"

"Why don't you both shut your mouths." Max walked through the front door, not bothering to knock, and glanced between Ivy and Jack. "What's going on?"

"Why is your front door unlocked, Ivy? I just told you that you had to be careful," Jack said. "You need to lock your door."

"You walked in behind me," Ivy reminded him. "I was trying to lock you out when you forced your way in. It's your fault the door isn't locked."

Max narrowed his eyes. "What do you mean he forced his way in?"

"I tried to shut the door and he wouldn't let me." Ivy was suddenly prim and proper, although there was a gleam in her eye. If Jack didn't know better, he would think she was having a good time fighting with him.

"You forced your way into my sister's house?" Max challenged, tossing his keys on the coffee table and stalking around the edge of the couch. Jack held his ground, even though he was worried Max would start throwing punches. He didn't blame the man for being upset.

"She was in pain from exerting her shoulder and I wanted to check on it," Jack said, holding up his hands and refusing to make any sudden moves. "I'm actually glad you're here. Your sister won't listen to reason. Maybe you will."

"Why would I possibly listen to anything you have to say?"

"Because ... Ivy could be in danger," Jack replied simply.

"You know who's going to be in danger? You," Max said. "You're a jackass."

"I may be a jackass ... okay, I'm definitely a jackass ... but that doesn't mean that Ivy isn't in danger," Jack said.

"You have exactly thirty seconds to tell me why that is," Max said. "After that I'm beating your ass."

"Make sure you take him outside to do it," Ivy called from the refrigerator. "I was shot. I shouldn't have to clean the house, too."

Jack frowned. "You shouldn't be making jokes about that. This is serious."

"Oh, you're turning it into a soap opera all on your own," Ivy replied. "I don't have the energy to get worked up."

Jack rolled his neck until it cracked and turned his attention back to Max. He explained about the ballistics match and what it meant, Max asking the appropriate questions and shooting the occasional worried look in Ivy's direction. Twenty minutes later, Max was all caught up.

"Is that it?"

"Isn't that enough?" Jack challenged.

"It's a mess," Max agreed. "I honestly hope you find who is doing this. Whoever it is wants to torture you. I feel bad for you."

"Don't feel bad for me," Jack said. "Just … take care of your sister."

"Oh, that's what I'm doing," Max said. "We need to take this outside now."

"What do you mean?"

"I have to kick your ass," Max explained. "She's my sister and you broke her heart. It's my job to kick you in your special place and make you cry."

"I already want to cry," Jack muttered, rubbing the back of his neck. He cast a forlorn look in Ivy's direction as she mixed something in a bowl behind the counter. "Watch her. Keep her safe."

"It's too late for that," Max said. "You already hurt her more than any bullet ever could."

"If you think I'm proud of that, I'm not," Jack said. "I can't … if something were to happen to her … ."

Max's expression softened before he caught himself. "I'm sorry. You still need an ass whooping."

Jack rolled his eyes. "Is that what will make you feel better? Your sister smacked me across the face earlier. She seemed to enjoy that."

"You're not bleeding so she obviously didn't do it hard enough."

"No one is going to fight," Ivy said, injecting herself into the conversation for the first time in almost a half hour. "It's done. Leave him alone, Max. He has enough on his mind."

"Are you honestly going to protect him?" Max was incensed.

"I'm honestly going to ... let him go," Ivy replied, wiping her hands off on a dishtowel and crossing the room. "You should probably go, Jack."

Jack's heart lurched. He knew what she was saying and it hurt. "Ivy, when this is over, we can start again. It will be better. I promise. I just ... I have to keep you safe. That's the one thing that I need to do above all else.

"Just give me a few days," he pleaded. "We can start again."

"We can't go back," Ivy said, her voice cracking. "You picked this as our outcome. You made the decision for both of us. You did this. Now you have to live with it because I can't let you break my heart twice. Now ... go."

Ten

❧❧❧

"Well, well, well. You don't look so bad for someone who was shot … other than that dirty look on your face."

Felicity Goodings studied Ivy from behind the counter of her magic shop the next morning. In truth, while Ivy was a beautiful girl, she looked downtrodden and miserable right now. That wasn't enhancing her beauty.

"Ha, ha. You're so funny I forgot to laugh." Ivy hopped up on one of the stools across from her aunt and let loose with a dramatic sigh that would only be welcome on a teenage television show.

"Is something wrong, dear?" Felicity tamped down her laughter. When she first heard Ivy was shot she was in her car and on the way to the hospital without giving it a second thought. She never had children of her own, so her sister's children became surrogates. She loved both Max and Ivy with her whole heart.

After talking to Max, though, he explained Ivy was in no mood to be smothered – at least by family – and it would be better to wait to see her. Felicity knew it would only be a matter of time before Ivy came to her.

They were kindred souls – even though Ivy refused to acknowledge the magical things sprouting up in her life – and Felicity was convinced Ivy was coming into her own as a witch. She would never tell her niece that, though. The girl wasn't ready for something like that.

"Why would anything be wrong?" Ivy asked, sarcasm practically dripping from her tongue. "My life is perfect. Haven't you heard?"

Felicity pursed her lips. Something was definitely going on here. "Why are you so depressed?"

"I was shot."

"I know you were shot. You were the lead story on the local news two days running."

Ivy knit her eyebrows together. "I was? I didn't know that. Did they use a photograph? I hate the way I look in photographs."

Felicity couldn't rein in her smile this time. Of course that would be the thing Ivy focused on. "They used a nice photo of you and Max," she said. "I believe your brother supplied it from his own personal stash. He looked very handsome in it."

Ivy scowled. "That means I probably looked goofy, doesn't it?"

"Actually you looked beautiful," Felicity countered. "It was taken last summer at the nursery. You had a beautiful skirt on, and a bright smile on your face. You're wearing neither today."

Ivy glanced down at her plain cargo pants and simple black shirt. "I'm not in the mood to dress up."

"I can see that," Felicity said. "Do you want to tell me what happened to inspire this mood?"

"Jack broke up with me."

Felicity wasn't sure if she heard her niece correctly. "I'm sorry ... what?"

"Jack dumped me," Ivy said matter-of-factly. "Actually, I'm not sure we actually got to that part. He waited with me in the hospital until Max showed up and then he just ... took off."

"I don't understand," Felicity said, confused. "Jack adores you. You two fight like you're going to rip each other's clothes off any second. Why would he do that?"

"He's done with me."

Felicity rolled her eyes. She could tell Ivy was feeling sorry for herself. The things she was saying about Jack made absolutely no sense, though. She'd seen the duo together. The atmosphere around them positively crackled when they were in the same room. "What did he say?"

"What does that matter?"

Felicity narrowed her eyes. She was in no mood for games. "Is Jack struggling because of what happened to him?" Despite her best intentions, Felicity accidentally got a gander at Jack's wretched past when she inadvertently read his aura weeks before. She promised to keep it to herself, but since Ivy already knew about the shooting she wasn't breaking any oaths. "You know it's probably hard for him to deal with a shooting when it happens to someone he cares about. You should have a little patience."

"Yes, this all my fault," Ivy deadpanned. "I did not come here to listen to you take up for poor Jack and his moody bag of tricks."

Felicity chuckled. She couldn't help herself. "Let me see if I understand what's going on," she suggested. "You got shot and Jack freaked out. Instead of doting on you like you thought he should, he disappeared to freak out on his own.

"You overreacted and cut him out of your life and now you're feeling sorry for yourself," she continued. "Does that about sum it up?"

"No."

"Then why don't you tell me how it happened while I pour you a soothing cup of tea," Felicity prodded. "I might slip a mood elevator in there, but that can only help right now."

Ivy rolled her eyes but launched into her story anyway. She didn't come to her aunt because she wanted the woman to take Jack's side. She came to her aunt because she needed a sounding board that wasn't Max, Michael, or Luna. When she was done, Felicity was more sympathetic.

"Well, I'm not going to pretend that Jack did the right thing," she said. "If you ask him how he feels about all of this, he's probably going to say he did everything wrong. Still … ."

"I knew you were going to take his side," Ivy hissed.

Felicity ignored her niece's outburst. "Still, Jack went through a horror that you cannot possibly relate to."

Ivy wordlessly gestured to her shoulder.

"Yes, a flesh wound that took seven stitches to close up is the same thing as several gunshot wounds to the chest, isn't it?"

Ivy made a face. "I'm not saying it's the same thing."

"What are you saying?"

Ivy was frustrated. "He promised he wasn't going to break my heart." The tears she'd managed to avoid all day threatened to return. "He promised not to purposely hurt me."

"Do you honestly think that's what he's doing?" Felicity asked, squeezing Ivy's hand to offer her reassurance. "Do you think Jack feels so little for you that he just tossed you away without a second thought?"

"That's exactly what I think."

"Then you're an idiot," Felicity said, refusing to mince words. "Jack is so enamored with you he can't see straight. He has been since you two sparred at your very first meeting. He fought his attraction to you as long as he could – failed miserably during the process – and then gave in because he was tortured without you.

"On your very first official date a cop was shot and Jack watched him die on the pavement," she continued. "He was already shaken up before you were injured. How do you think he felt watching you hit the ground right next to him?"

"Probably better than I felt."

"You're being a complete and total pain," Felicity grumbled. "Jack panicked. He didn't know what to do, so he panicked. It happens sometimes. I know you've put Jack up on some kind of a pedestal, but he's entitled to make a few mistakes. You're not exactly perfect yourself, my dear."

"I wouldn't have left him if he was shot."

"You're not haunted by the same memories Jack is," Felicity reminded her. "You saw his dreams. You saw what he survived – and how he tortured himself with the memories. Don't you think he's doing the same thing now?"

Ivy worried her bottom lip with her teeth, conflicted. She'd been pushing those very thoughts out of her mind because it was easier to hate Jack than have empathy for him. If she understood his plight, if she gave in to the sympathy, then she would be right back where she started. "It hurts to think about him."

"I'm sure it hurts him to think about you, too," Felicity said. "He has guilt about your shooting plaguing him. He blames himself because whoever did this is going after you to punish him. He's dealing with a lot more than you are right now."

"He still broke my heart."

"Or perhaps he merely delayed your happy ending," Felicity suggested. "You two are not going to be able to stay away from each other no matter what. Jack may think he's protecting you, but he'll be back because you're the only thing keeping him sane."

"Well, that's a sad commentary on his mental fortitude."

"You make me laugh, girl," Felicity said, snickering. "We both know that you're going to forgive Jack once he gets his head out of his rear end. Instead of working against him, why don't you try helping him so you can get this nastiness behind you and have a better picnic."

Ivy stilled. "What do you mean?"

"Ivy, I think you're missing a very important piece of this puzzle," Felicity said. "The gun used to shoot Jack ... and the police officer in Bellaire ... and you ... was thought to have burned up in the same fiery car crash that claimed Jack's former partner."

"How do you know that?"

"I called Brian because I wanted information on your shooting," Felicity replied, not missing a beat.

"So you knew about all of this before I told you? Why did you make me go through the entire story again?"

"Because I wanted to see what kind of spin you put on it. You could be a human carousel."

"Oh, whatever," Ivy muttered, crossing her arms over her chest. "If that gun was supposed to be destroyed, how did someone get it?"

Felicity internally chuckled. Ivy was finally thinking things through clearly. "That's one of the important questions we need answers to," she conceded. "The other one involves Jack's partner. This is obviously retribution for what happened in Detroit. Someone is sending Jack a message, although we can't be sure what it is yet. So, what we need to ask ourselves is who loved Jack's partner enough to want revenge?"

"Huh." Ivy was lost in thought. She hated it when her aunt was right. "How can we find out the answers to those questions?"

Felicity's eyes twinkled. "I was hoping you would ask that. I have an idea."

JACK SUCKED IN A DEEP BREATH AND THEN PUNCHED IN LAURA Simmons' phone number. He hadn't seen the amiable woman since her brother shot him and left him for dead in the street. She didn't come to see him in the hospital – although he didn't blame her for that – and he didn't go to Marcus' funeral.

They met several times throughout his three-year partnership with Marcus, mostly at family barbecues and the like. She'd always been pleasant, if a little scattered, and a few times Jack worried she developed a crush on him. He didn't think that would be a problem this time.

"Hello."

"Laura?"

"Yes, this is Laura. Who is this?"

Jack had only a split-second to decide if he was going to retreat. When Ivy's sad face flitted through his mind, he forced himself to be strong. "It's Jack Harker."

There was silence on the other end of the phone for a full thirty seconds. Jack was almost convinced she hung up on him when she found her voice. "I ... wow, Jack. It's been a long time."

"It has," Jack agreed. "I ... um ... how have you been?" As much as he wanted to get straight to the point he knew he would turn Laura off if he immediately started grilling her on the disposition of her brother's body and what happened to his personal belongings.

"I'm okay," Laura said. "It's been ... difficult ... but I'm managing. How are you? I heard you moved."

"I did," Jack said. "I moved to a small town called Shadow Lake. It's in the northwestern part of the lower peninsula."

"That sounds ... very different ... from what you were doing down here."

"I needed something different," Jack said. "I needed a change. I needed a place where the pressure was lessened."

"Did you find that in Shadow Lake?"

"I did."

"Well, I'm happy for you," Laura said. "Listen, Jack, I probably should've come to see you in the hospital after what happened. After Marcus died, it didn't seem right and my mother was having trouble understanding everything the cops were saying. She didn't believe he could possibly be guilty. It was a horrible time."

"I understand that, Laura. I didn't expect you to visit me. I wasn't really in the mood to see people."

"I'm sure you weren't. I still should've made the effort to come and see you. It was just too hard."

"It was hard on all of us," Jack said, his discomfort rising. This was not what he wanted to talk about. "Laura, I didn't just call to catch up on old times. I need to know what happened to your brother's body after the explosion."

Silence.

"Laura?"

"That's a really strange question, Jack."

"I'm sorry," Jack offered. "There's been a spot of trouble up here ... two shootings in fact ... and the ballistics came back as a match for Marcus' gun. I need to know how that's possible."

"I'm not sure I have an answer for you, Jack. I never even wondered about what happened to his gun. I always assumed it burned up with him in the fire."

"I did, too," Jack said. "It doesn't seem to be the case, though. What about Marcus' body?"

"You don't think he's behind this, do you?" Laura asked. "I can assure you that he died in that fire. They ran dental records."

"I don't think it's him," Jack clarified. "I'm just getting all of my ducks in a row."

"Well, he was cremated," Laura explained. "He was burned pretty badly and they recommended we not see him ... so we didn't. We had him cremated and my mother put his ashes in an urn. It's on the mantle above her fireplace."

"And you have no idea what happened to his gun?"

"I'm sorry, Jack. I don't."

"Well, I didn't expect you to know," Jack said. "I had to give it a shot, though. I'm sorry to have bugged you. I'm glad you're doing okay. I hope things continue to get better for you."

"You, too."

Eleven

"This is the dumbest idea you've ever had." Ivy glanced around her aunt's small living room with a disgusted look on her face. "Seriously? How can you possibly think this is a good idea?"

Felicity reminded herself that Ivy was recuperating from a trauma – the one to her heart more painful than the one to her body – and continued lighting candles in a circle around her niece. "Do you have a better idea?"

"Than a séance? Yeah, I think I can come up with a few."

"What are they?"

Ivy stilled. "What do you mean?"

"If you can come up with a few ideas that are better than a séance, I would love to hear what they are."

Ivy licked her lips. "Well … we could drive down to Detroit and question Marcus Simmons' family members."

"That sounds like a great way to get shot … again."

"They're the ones who will know what happened to his things," Ivy pointed out. "They're the ones who know any girlfriends … or friends … who would care about Marcus enough to kill in the name of his memory."

"Have you considered that one of those family members might be the guilty party?"

"Huh."

"I didn't think so," Felicity said, biting her cheek to keep from laughing. Ivy was a smart girl, but when she decided she didn't want to do something she was something of a terror. "We can't go knocking on random people's doors. Some of those people are in legitimate mourning. No matter what their son did, they weren't responsible for his actions."

"Fine." Ivy crossed her arms over her chest.

"Someone might also know who you are on sight and shoot you," Felicity added. "They probably won't miss a second time."

"I said fine," Ivy snapped. "It's just ... we haven't done this since I was fourteen and you chaperoned that sleepover. Do you remember what happened that night?"

Felicity smiled at the memory. "I believe your friends accused me of being a witch and you got angry and kicked them all out," she said. "Then we ate ice cream and watched *The Shining*."

"Yeah, I've always loved that movie."

"It's a classic," Felicity agreed. "I remember that night being fun, even if you did have a minor meltdown."

"According to you I always have a minor meltdown."

"Oh, sometimes they're not minor," Felicity said. "That's why I think you should probably calm down a little bit and give Jack a chance to get over his own meltdown before you heap more of yours on him."

"I get it. You love Jack."

"I don't think I'm the only one," Felicity shot back, her eyes twinkling.

"I don't love Jack," Ivy protested, flabbergasted. "We've only known each other for a month."

"And yet your hearts have already joined. I find that ... refreshing."

"I think you're delusional," Ivy retorted. "I don't love Jack."

"Okay."

"I don't," Ivy said. "I'm attracted to him. There's a difference."

"Fine," Felicity conceded. "You don't love Jack. You're merely on your way to loving Jack. I stand corrected."

"I really dislike you sometimes."

Felicity smiled. "Shall we get this show on the road? If you're going to freak out, I'd at least like you to see a ghost before you do it."

"Oh, whatever," Ivy muttered. "I don't believe in ghosts."

Felicity settled herself on the floor across from Ivy, grabbing her niece's hands and making a circle with their arms. "Did you believe in dream walking before it happened?"

Ivy faltered. "No."

"You have magic inside of you, Ivy Morgan," Felicity said. "You just have to let it out. If you didn't believe in dream walking, but it turned out to be real, isn't there a chance there's something else out there after death?"

"I guess," Ivy conceded. "I really don't want to meet a murderous ghost, though. It's going to be really hard to be nice to the guy who shot Jack."

"Who says you have to be nice to him?"

"I don't think being mean to him is going to get us anywhere," Ivy said.

"Oh, good point," Felicity said, squeezing Ivy's hands. "Now, close your eyes. Try to relax. Don't think about anything but Marcus Simmons."

"Oh, well, great. Now I want to throw up."

"Zip it, Ivy."

Ivy sighed, resigned. She did as her aunt asked and closed her eyes, shifting uncomfortably for a few minutes until her mind started to wander. The scent of the candles combined with her aunt's calming presence allowed her busy mind to relax.

"Marcus Simmons, we're calling to you," Felicity intoned. "We command that you cross over to this side."

Nothing happened.

Felicity tried again. "Marcus Simmons, if you're out there, you need to come to us," she said. "We have questions only you can answer. You owe this world something. We're here to collect."

Ivy internally snickered. That sounded ominous. She was just about to give up and suggest going for ice cream when the candles around them started flickering. She was supposed to have her eyes closed, but the unmistakable "sizzle" forced her to make sure they weren't accidentally going to burn her aunt's apartment to the ground.

"Aunt Felicity?"

"Shh," Felicity admonished. "He's here."

"How do you know that?" Ivy was curious. She didn't feel anything out of the ordinary in the room.

"I know," Felicity said. "I ... ." She cocked her head to the side, wrinkling her nose. "Do you feel that?"

Ivy decided to completely give herself over to the process. She pressed her eyes shut again, reaching out with her mind until ... that was impossible. Ivy's eyes flew open, fear coursing through her. "Aunt Felicity ... ."

"I felt it, too," Felicity said, calming Ivy with the sound of her voice. "It's okay."

It wasn't okay, though. Ivy felt another presence. Something was in the room. Something was watching them. Without thinking about what she was doing, she jerked her hands away from Felicity and rolled out of the circle, her face ashen.

"Why did you do that?" Felicity chided. "We were getting somewhere."

"I know we were getting somewhere," Ivy hissed. "I felt ... her."

Felicity stilled. "Her? I thought Jack's partner was a man."

"Marcus Simmons was definitely a man," Ivy said. "What we just came in contact with was not, though. It was something else."

"Are you sure?" Felicity was dubious. "I didn't get close enough to feel a gender. How did you?"

"I have no idea," Ivy said, pushing herself to her feet. "I just know that I'm done ... doing this ... and I'm going home."

"Ivy, we can't give up now," Felicity pressed. "That ghost was drawn to us for a reason. She might have the answers we're looking for."

"I don't care," Ivy said, shaking her head. "I ... I'm sorry. I can't do this. It's too much." She turned on her heel and hurried out of the apartment, slamming the door behind her and not risking a backward glance at her disappointed aunt.

Felicity watched her go with quiet contemplation. Perhaps Ivy was even stronger than she originally thought. If Ivy could feel something she couldn't, that meant Ivy was more advanced than anyone realized.

"Well, that's mighty interesting," Felicity muttered. "Too bad she couldn't hold off her meltdown until we actually contacted a ghost. She always ruins my fun."

"DO YOU HAVE ANYTHING?" BRIAN ASKED, DROPPING A DELI BAG on Jack's desk and moving to his own before settling.

Jack eyed the bag suspiciously. "Did you spit in my food?"

"No."

"Did you have the girl who made it spit in it?"

"No," Brian replied. "Thanks for giving me the idea for next time, though."

Jack sighed as he yanked a hand through his messy hair. He had nervous energy and he'd expended it by tugging his hands through his hair every thirty seconds for the past two hours. "I feel like I'm going in circles."

"Laura Simmons didn't give you anything?"

"She said her brother was cremated and that she had no idea his gun was even missing until I told her about the shootings here," Jack replied, digging into the bag. He wasn't really hungry on the surface, but his growling stomach told him he should eat something. He bit into the roast beef sandwich and made a face.

"I honestly didn't have anyone spit in your food," Brian said. "I'm not twelve."

"It's not that," Jack said. "It's just … Ivy's was better."

"Oh, good grief," Brian grumbled. "Are you going to spend the next week mooning over Ivy?"

"Probably."

"Why don't you go to her house, fall to your knees, and beg her to take you back instead? That way we can focus on the case instead of your lovesick heart. How does that sound?"

It sounded exactly like what Jack wanted to do. That didn't mean he *should* do it. "I can't do that until I know she won't be in danger because of me," he said.

"Have you considered that she's already a target and that putting distance between the two of you is only going to make her easier to get to?" Brian asked.

Jack balked. "No. Why would you think that?"

"Everyone knows you were together up until … this," Brian said. "That's all anyone can talk about."

"I didn't realize I was so popular."

"It's not you," Brian clarified. "Ivy Morgan has been the 'girl to get' for years. Every man in her age group has tried and she shot them all down. You're the only one to get close to her since … well, it's been a really long time."

"That makes me feel worse."

"Good," Brian said. "I talked to her the other day. Did she tell you that?"

"We were too busy fighting … and then sleeping … and then fighting some more," Jack replied. "I knew someone told her what happened. I figured it was you."

"You slept together?" Brian was stunned. "You broke up with her and then slept with her? What kind of deviant are you?"

"We didn't sleep together *that* way," Jack hissed. "That's none of your business, by the way. We just … Ivy took her painkillers and they knocked her out. I was tired from the hangover so I kind of … slept next to her."

"Oh, well, that makes it perfectly all right," Brian said, nonplussed. "By the way, it is my business because I happen to love Ivy. As long as you're going to be moody and pining for her it affects our partnership. Suck it up."

"I'm not pining for her."

"Son, if you were pining any harder you would turn into a literal tree," Brian countered. "I'm not joking with you. I think we're kind of stuck here because you can't think outside the box as long as Ivy is on your mind."

"I won't put her in danger," Jack snapped. "What kind of man does that?"

"Jack, she's already in danger," Brian argued. "Just because you decided to dump her in the dirt like a jackass, that doesn't mean whoever is after you cares. She's still a target."

Jack's heart rolled. Was that true? Was he making things worse by staying away from her? Could he keep her safe if he was close?

"Just think about it," Brian prodded. "Finish the rest of your sandwich. If we're lucky your stomach will outsmart your brain and go running to Ivy for comfort."

Jack chuckled hoarsely. "Maybe."

"Make sure you beg her good," Brian said. "She's going to be mean as all get out to you when you go crawling back. I think we both know you deserve it, but she's going to take a lot of convincing."

"That's what I'm afraid of."

IVY WAS SHAKEN WHEN SHE LEFT FELICITY'S. SHE KNEW IT WAS juvenile to run out on her aunt like that, but she couldn't get the feeling of "touching" something she knew shouldn't be there out of her head. She'd never experienced anything like it. She could hardly process what she was feeling.

Her mind was muddled for the duration of the ride back to Shadow Lake. Ivy couldn't get her hands to stop shaking until she pulled onto the road that led to her cottage.

She was anxious to get home. She wanted to lock the doors, grab a blanket, and curl up with Nicodemus and a good book so she could close out the rest of the world for a few hours. She was almost to her driveway when a loud "bang" jolted her. She didn't have time to focus on it, though, because her car careened toward the ditch in front of her house.

Ivy couldn't control the car, and she was thankful there was no oncoming traffic when she sailed across both lanes and into the ditch. Her momentary feeling of relief didn't last long when she realized what happened: Someone shot out her tire.

Twelve

"What about Simmons' mother?" Brian asked, opening his bag of potato chips. "Would she be willing to talk to you?"

Jack shrugged. "I honestly don't know," he answered, pushing his potato salad around the container. It didn't look half as good as Ivy's had the previous day. "Janet was a good woman. She was always nice to me. She used to bring in a homemade lunch for us once a week, and she always teased me about finding a woman to settle down with."

"Well, you've done that," Brian said. "You just have to get her to forgive you."

Jack scowled. "Do you have to keep bringing up Ivy? It's bad enough that I can't stop thinking about how much better her potato salad was … or how much better her sandwich was … or how much I miss her smile. You're making this worse."

"Ugh. You're wrecked, son. Give in and do the right thing. You're not going to feel better until you do."

"And what happens if Ivy dies because I can't stand to be without her?"

"What happens if she dies because you were being a horse's ass and staying away from her?" Brian challenged.

"I … ."

The sound of Brian's desk phone ringing cut off Jack's answer, saving him from the prospect of having to admit he was desperate to do exactly what Brian suggested. "Saved by the bell," Brian muttered, lifting the receiver. "Brian Nixon."

Jack watched his partner, the man's eyes narrowing and causing Jack to straighten in his chair. Something was going on.

"Ivy, slow down," Brian ordered, causing Jack's heart to roll.

"Is that Ivy? Give me that phone." Jack reached for it, but Brian pushed his chair back and slapped Jack's greedy hand away.

"Are you sure that's what happened?" Brian asked, his tone grave. "Where are you now? Okay. No … Ivy, do not get out of that vehicle. Make yourself small and get down as close to the floor of the car as you can. I'm on my way. I'll be there as fast as I can. Don't risk getting out of that car and trying to run to your house. You'll only make yourself an easier target."

Brian disconnected and jumped to his feet. "We have to go."

"What happened?" Jack felt as if he was swimming in quicksand.

"Someone shot out Ivy's tire and caused her to fly into the ditch by her house," he said. "She's okay … the front window shattered … but she's exposed. We have to get out there."

IVY WASN'T HAVING THE BEST DAY. BETWEEN LOSING JACK, feeling a ghost brush up against her, having to listen to her aunt extol all of Jack's virtues, and now being shot at … again … she was pretty much at her limit.

She heard a vehicle approach from her spot on the car floor, but she was too terrified to look up. When the driver's side door flew open, Ivy instinctively covered her face. The next thing she knew she was being hauled out of the car and into Jack's arms.

Jack cried out when he saw her, pressing his face against hers as he rocked her. He'd almost convinced himself she would be dead by the time they got to her. He was sure he'd never get a chance to apologize. "Honey … I … ."

He was crying. For a second Ivy couldn't understand why he was shaking. That's when she realized what was happening. "I'm okay, Jack. I'm … shaken up, but I'm okay."

Jack sobbed as he held her, opening his mouth to offer her reassuring words and yet finding none.

"Jack, you're smothering her," Brian said, tugging on his partner's arm. "Let her breathe."

Jack refused to relinquish his grasp.

"It's okay," Ivy said, her expression rueful. "It's probably the best thing that's happened to me all day. How sad is that?"

Brian offered her a sympathetic smirk, but the expression didn't make it all the way up to his eyes. "You're cut up a little on your cheek there, kid. Does anything else hurt?"

Ivy shifted her eyes to Jack. "Just my heart."

After a few more minutes of incoherent crying, Jack finally released his grip on Ivy so he could walk her back to the cottage. Brian moved with them to the front porch, his eyes alert, but then he left them to a few moments of privacy as he moved back out to the road to take care of Ivy's vehicle and wait for backup.

Jack checked Ivy's house to make sure it was empty, Nicodemus shooting him a disdainful look as he waited next to his food bowl, and then Jack turned his full attention to Ivy. "Let me see your face."

Ivy's hand flew up to her cheek, flinching when she made contact with the cut. "Well, I guess this is the frosting on top of the cupcake of my day."

Jack pressed his lips together. "It's not bad. I'll clean it up and make sure there's not any glass in it, but … it won't scar or anything."

"That's good," Ivy quipped. "It's going to be hard enough to get a man when I have pink hair and a gunshot wound. When you add a disfigured face into the mix, I'm going to be considered the new hunchback of Shadow Lake."

"I don't want you to say that." Jack swallowed hard. "I … ."

"Oh, lighten up, Jack," Ivy chided. "If now isn't the time for inappropriate dating humor, when is?"

"I don't want you joking about dating anyone else," Jack admitted. "I … we're going to fix this and then you're going to be dating me. I don't like to share."

"How are we going to fix this, Jack?" Ivy challenged. "You don't want to be with me. I'm not going to force you to do something you're uncomfortable with. We're ... done."

"Shut up and sit on the table," Jack instructed, striding down her hallway so he could gather her first aid kit from the bathroom – and his nerve. When he returned to the kitchen, he was surprised to find her doing exactly what he asked. "I guess you're more shaken up than you want to admit, huh? You're actually doing something I told you to do. It must be a day for miracles."

"Yeah, I'm feeling pretty miraculous," Ivy sniped. "I spent the morning with my aunt and listened to her tell me that I was giving you a raw deal. Then she tried to conduct a séance to talk to Marcus Simmons' ghost. Then I got shot at and wrecked my car on my way home. That's miraculous for sure."

Jack frowned as he dabbed peroxide on a cotton ball. "What do you mean when you say she tried to do a séance?"

"Oh, well, she lit candles and told Marcus he had some explaining to do and then ... well ... I left and came home because it was all so ridiculous." There was no way Ivy was going to admit to brushing up against a ghost. She was already in a vulnerable position. There was no need to exacerbate it.

Jack gently touched the cotton ball to Ivy's cheek, his eyes locking with hers. "What did you see when you were coming home?"

"Nothing."

"Are you sure?"

Ivy nodded. "I was kind of lost in my head," she admitted. "I wasn't paying attention."

"It was the front driver's side tire that was shot out," Jack said. "That means the shot came from your left. Try to think. Did you see any movement ... maybe something you brushed off as an animal or something ... or did you see a person?"

"Yes, Jack. I saw a person and failed to mention it after I got shot at. Whoops."

Jack sighed. Brian was right about her being angry. Now was not the time for petulance, though. "I'm just trying to ... protect you. I'm trying to get answers so we can find out who is doing this. Then we can ... ."

"Don't finish that sentence," Ivy warned, wagging a finger in Jack's face. "You either want to be with me or you don't. I'm pretty sure that leaving me in the hospital after I was shot means you don't. It's ... okay."

Jack pressed his eyes shut. "Ivy ... ."

"I'm sorry I've been ragging on you," Ivy offered. "I can't explain it. It's not fair. Technically we had one date. I'm being mean to you over one date. I have no idea what's wrong with me."

Jack knew what was wrong with her. It was the same thing eating away at him. "We've had more than one date," he corrected. "We've had quite a few of them in our dreams. I already know you better than anyone else I've ever been with."

"Yes, but that wasn't real, was it?" Ivy asked, her voice cracking.

"It sure felt real," Jack replied. "I ... this is all my fault. If you think I'm not taking responsibility, then you're wrong. I have no idea who is doing this. I'm so desperate to keep you safe that I'm putting you in danger. I ... don't know what to do."

"You don't have to do anything," Ivy said. "You made your decision. I'm the one who has to live with it. I kept telling myself that you would regret it, but ... ."

"I do regret it," Jack rasped out. "I regret leaving you at the hospital. I regret getting drunk and spending six straight hours watching your back in a dream. I regret fighting with you ... and scaring you ... and hurting you. I regret all of it."

Ivy stilled. "When did you watch my back in a dream?"

"You were in your fairy ring the night of the shooting. I drank because I didn't want you to find me in our dreams. I found you, though. I was too afraid to approach you because of what I did."

"I felt you," Ivy murmured, her blue eyes stormy. "I told myself I was imagining it because I was such a wreck when I finally fell asleep. I wouldn't turn around because I was afraid you weren't really there. I wanted to comfort myself with the delusion that you were watching over me."

"It wasn't a delusion," Jack countered. "I did watch you. I was a coward, but I watched you."

Ivy bit the inside of her cheek. "You realize that I'm still a target whether you're with me or not, right?"

Jack nodded.

"I don't want you to protect me out of a sense of obligation," Ivy said. "I want you to want me."

"Oh, honey, I want you more than I've ever wanted anything," Jack said. "I'm so scared that I'm going to screw this up, though. I need to know you're safe before we can move beyond this – and I desperately want to move beyond this. I need to know that my past isn't going to kill our future. Do you understand that?"

"I guess I do," Ivy conceded. "I need something from you, though."

"Name it."

"I need you to go," Ivy said, causing Jack's heart to flop. "I need you to leave. I don't want you to come back here until you're sure that I'm what you want."

Jack opened his mouth to argue, but Ivy shushed him with a look.

"You can say you want me, but I don't think it's true," Ivy said. "It hurts to feel like I'm the one doing all of the caring while you do all of the walking away. I don't want to let you go, but I'm afraid it will kill me to try and hold onto you when you don't want to stay.

"So, I want you to go," she continued. "If you come back here, you have to be ready to be with me. Make sure that's what you want. I can't go through this again. I can't be with someone I don't trust, and if you keep walking away from me I'll never be able to trust you."

"Ivy … ."

"No," Ivy said, cutting him off. "You have some thinking to do. You have a decision to make. I've already made mine. I want you, Jack, but I don't want you walking in and out of my life whenever you feel like it.

"You're either with me or you're not," Ivy said, her voice firm. "Make a choice."

Thirteen

"How is Ivy?" Brian asked, scanning Jack's pale face as his partner joined him by the road.

"She's okay."

"How are you?"

"I'm ... I don't know," Jack answered, his mind busy. "I have no idea. She's so strong. I'm a coward and she's a hero. I don't know what to do."

"You know what to do," Brian countered. "You're right about being a coward, though. That's why you're out here with me instead of in there making things right with her."

Jack ran a hand through his hair, yanking on it for good measure to draw him back to reality. "How bad is her car?"

"I'm having it towed to the garage in town," Brian replied, knowing Jack needed to talk about the investigation as a front so he could internally wrap his head around whatever went down with Ivy inside of her house. "I don't think it's too bad. She's going to need a new tire and windshield ... and she'll probably need a front-end alignment ... but she got off lucky."

"Did she?"

"What do you mean?"

"What if whoever is doing this isn't trying to kill her but scare her away from me," Jack suggested. "Both of the shots had to come from some distance ... and with a handgun ... that means whoever this is has training. If they're that good, they should be able to deliver a kill shot. They certainly wouldn't miss twice."

"I think there's merit to that theory," Brian said.

Jack nodded, relieved Brian had faith in his pronouncement.

"I also think you're floating it because it gives you a reason not to run back to Ivy and get what you want," Brian added.

"But ... ."

Brian shook his head. "It doesn't matter if this person is trying to kill her or not," he said. "She could've died from the impact if she hit a tree. She could've moved her face at the last minute and took that bullet in the cheek and died in the middle of your picnic. No matter how you try to justify staying away from her, she's a target."

"I know." Jack glanced back at the house, wishing Ivy would at least stand in the window so he could see her.

"Jack, you said yourself that you're being a coward," Brian said, choosing his words carefully. "Stop being a coward. Be a man. Go get your girl."

Jack didn't need to be told twice.

IVY WAS ANNOYED WHEN SHE HEARD THE INSISTENT KNOCKING on her front door. She tried to ignore it, visions of sinking into a steaming bath flitting through her head, but whoever was out there wasn't leaving.

She gripped her robe against her chest, being careful it wouldn't fly open and traumatize the person knocking, and wrenched open the door. "I'm fine. I ... ."

She didn't get a chance to finish her sentence because Jack pushed his way into her house, kicking the door shut behind him with his foot and cupping her face with his hands so he could draw her close.

"Jack, I told you that I didn't want you to come back until you decided what you want."

"I have decided," Jack replied. "I decided weeks ago, but I was too scared to admit it. I don't want to live my life afraid for one more second. I want you."

Ivy's heart pounded as she tried to grasp his words. "But ... ."

"No. No more 'buts.' No more 'what ifs.' No more 'we'll make this work down the road.' We're making it work now. I can't be without you. I don't want to try. This is what I want."

"I can't take it if you walk away from me again." Ivy's eyes filled with tears. "I can't. It's just going to get harder every time you walk away from me and it already hurt so much I could barely breathe this time."

"I won't walk away," Jack promised. "I can't because it hurts too much to be away from you. I want to be with you."

"You say that now. What happens when you decide you need to protect me again?"

"Then we're going to fight," Jack said, rubbing his thumb against Ivy's cheek. "It's a good thing we're both good at it."

"What happens when you decide you have to leave me for my own good?" Ivy almost choked on the words.

"That won't happen again," Jack said. "I can't be away from you for *my* own good. I ... ache ... when I'm away from you. I'm sorry for hurting you. I'm sorry for making you doubt me – and yourself – by being an idiot. I won't do it again. Please ... give me one more chance."

"I ... ." Ivy pressed her lips together, unsure. Her head was telling her to kick him out because he would hurt her again. The next time she might not be able to recover. Her heart, though, that was a different story. "If you try to leave me again I'll hunt you down and kill you."

Jack laughed as he pulled her closer. "Right back at you." He didn't give her a chance to argue ... or change her mind. He slammed his mouth against hers, need overwhelming him. He lifted her off the ground, holding her flush against his chest with one arm as he double-checked to make sure the door was locked with his free hand. Then he walked down the hallway, not stopping until he reached her bedroom.

He knew with absolute certainty that he would never walk away from her again. Now it was time to get everything he ever wanted and prove to her that he could be everything she would ever need.

"THAT WAS ... PRETTY INTERESTING," IVY SAID, BRUSHING HER hair away from her face as she rested her chin on Jack's bare chest an hour later. "I ... ."

Jack slapped his hand over her mouth. "This is not a time for talking, honey."

Ivy narrowed her eyes and pushed his hand away. "Excuse me, but did you just tell me to shut up?"

"No," Jack said, tracing lazy circles across the back of her neck, marveling at the softness of her skin. "I was just hoping we could have five minutes of silence so I can sear what we just did into my memory forever. It doesn't get better than that."

Ivy snorted. "Oh, please. I have an injured shoulder. You should see what I can do when I'm at full strength."

Jack cocked a dubious eyebrow. "Really?"

"I guess you'll have to wait to find out," Ivy said, snuggling a little closer and running her finger over his defined abs. "Jack?"

"Hmm."

"Are you going to leave now?"

Jack sighed. He deserved that. "I'm not leaving, Ivy. I told you I wouldn't. I meant it."

"What about your investigation? Don't you have to ... I don't know ... go back and file a report?"

"Oh," Jack said, chuckling as he glanced down at her. "You were asking if I had to go back to work, weren't you?"

Ivy nodded.

"I thought you were asking if I was going to run out on you," Jack admitted. "For the record, the answer to both of those questions is no. Even if I didn't know how great ... this ... was going to be, now that I know I'm already addicted."

Ivy snickered. "I'm going to take that as a compliment."

"You definitely should," Jack said, pressing a soft kiss to Ivy's forehead. "Don't worry. Brian knew why I was coming back to the house. He's not expecting me at the office again until tomorrow."

"It's almost dark," Ivy murmured. "Have you eaten dinner?"

"No. I had a crappy sandwich for lunch. All I could think about was your sandwich and then I spent the rest of the meal feeling sorry for myself ... well, that and listening to Brian make fun of me because I was pining for you. Why? Are you hungry?"

"I don't know."

"You don't know if you're hungry? I guess I'm going to take that as a compliment since my sexual prowess – and pathetic neediness and apology – slapped the desire for food right out of you."

Ivy rolled her eyes. "I don't want to leave this bed. I want to be able to stay here for the rest of the night and ... feel ... you." She risked a glance at Jack to see if he was laughing, but his eyes were somber as they locked onto hers.

"We can stay here," he said. "I don't want to go anywhere else either. I need you to try and ... trust me, though. I know it's hard after what I did. I promise I won't leave you again."

"Jack, I do trust you," Ivy said. "I know you didn't mean to hurt me. It was still painful, though. You're probably lucky you didn't answer your phone ... or show up after the fact ... that night. Max was ready to kill you. He can't handle it when I cry."

"Max isn't the only one," Jack said, carefully tugging Ivy's slight frame so she was positioned on top of him and he could snuggle her closer. He was so comfortable, so thankful she was willing to give him another chance, he would gladly crawl into her skin with her if he could. "I don't ever want to make you cry."

"Well, you should know that the movie *E.T.* always makes me cry," Ivy admitted. "I can't help it."

"That's good to know. I'll burn every copy I find."

"Can you wait until morning for breakfast? I promise to fix you a big one," Ivy said, stifling a yawn.

"All I want to do is sleep," Jack admitted. "Do you need painkillers before I pass out? Tell me now. I'm exhausted."

"My heart doesn't hurt."

"What about your shoulder ... or back? You hit that ditch pretty hard."

"Nothing hurts," Ivy replied, her eyes shining. "I feel ... happy."

"I feel happy, too, honey," Jack said, kissing her softly. "I'm a little worried I'm going to drag you into a nightmare, but I've never been this happy. I need you to know that."

"And you'll be here when I wake up, right?" Ivy hated asking the question, but she needed reassurance.

"I will be here when you wake up," Jack said. "I won't move. I'll hold you all night. That's all I want."

"Okay." Ivy brushed her lips against his jaw. "The good news for you is that my shoulder will be fine in our dreams. When we do it again there you'll be able to see how good I really am."

Jack laughed, weariness lifting for a brief moment. "Now I really want to go to sleep."

"Goodnight, Jack."

"Goodnight, honey. I'll see you soon."

JACK KNEW HE WAS DREAMING BEFORE HE SAW THE BEACH, HIS heart soaring when he caught sight of Ivy's pink hair gleaming under the moonlight.

"This is new," Jack said, glancing around. "It's a different beach and we're here after dark. Where are we now?"

"I have no idea," Ivy answered. "I think it's a beach from a brochure I once saw."

"Not that I'm complaining, but I thought for sure I was going to force you into a bad place before you could drag us to a better place," Jack said. "This is a much happier outcome."

"It is," Ivy agreed. "I think I can control our destinations when I really put some effort into it. If you don't like this place, I can pick a new one."

"This place is perfect," Jack said, reaching for her. She was wearing a filmy beach cover up even though there was no sun to burn her delicate skin. "Are you wearing a bikini under that? Is that my reward for begging?"

94

Ivy snorted. "No."

"Oh." Jack was disappointed. "Now that I've seen all of your body I was hoping you would show off a little more skin."

Ivy broke into a wide smile and pointed at the placid ocean in front of them. "That's what the water is for."

Realization dawned on Jack and he felt a shiver of anticipation course through his body. "Is that where you're going to show me what you've got?"

"Of course," Ivy said, reaching for the beach cover-up. "I figured I'd give you a little preview before we go skinny-dipping in the real world."

"Oh, honey, that's the best thing I've ever heard."

Jack followed her into the water, being careful not to step on the cover-up even though he knew it wasn't real. It felt real. The emotions behind it were real. That was all that really mattered.

Fourteen

Ivy woke to warmth. She was still on top of Jack, his arms wrapped around her as he slumbered peacefully beneath her. He looked like one of those angel statues carved out of stone she'd seen in photography books. He was breathtaking.

"If you keep staring at me like that I'm going to charge you a fee," Jack teased, stretching.

"I thought you were asleep."

"I was … kind of," Jack murmured. "I'm too warm and comfortable to move, so I've been zoning out."

"You look handsome in the morning."

Jack wrenched his eyes open and focused on Ivy for the first time that day. "You don't look so bad yourself."

Ivy made a face that caused Jack to smirk. "I have bedhead," she replied. "Men wake up looking better than when they went to sleep and women wake up looking like train wrecks."

"I think you look cute," Jack countered, cupping the back of her head so he could kiss her. It was a soft gesture, simple, and yet it caused Ivy's heart rate to speed up. "What time is it?" he asked.

"Probably about the time you need to get up so you can go to work." Ivy wasn't happy with the prospect.

"Probably," Jack agreed, although he showed no signs of moving. "I'm not sure how I'm supposed to leave the happiest place on earth."

Ivy pursed her lips but couldn't entirely swallow her smile. "That's probably the best thing you could've said."

Jack snuggled her close again, relishing how her body fit against his so perfectly. "I can call Brian and tell him I'll be late. He'll understand. He'll give me endless grief about it, but he'll understand. We can spend the next three hours exactly like this and then face the day."

Ivy lifted her head. "We can't stay like this for three hours."

"Well, I thought we might do a little something else, too," Jack teased, tickling her ribs.

"That sounds nice," Ivy said, skirting his grip. "We can't do that right now either, though."

Jack didn't bother to hide his disappointment. "Why not?"

"Because if you don't stop holding me so tightly I'm going to have an accident," Ivy admitted. "We haven't moved in ten hours. Nature is calling."

Jack grinned. He couldn't help himself. She was the cutest thing he'd ever laid eyes on. "Well, then I guess I should let you go and do your thing while I start breakfast," he said. "We'll catch up on that other stuff after we fuel up."

"Deal."

IVY JOINED JACK IN THE KITCHEN TEN MINUTES LATER, HER FACE freshly washed and her hair brushed. Jack shook his head when he realized what else she did in the bathroom, until she planted a huge kiss on his lips.

"I see you brushed your teeth," Jack said, grinning when they separated. "Perhaps I should do you the honor of reciprocating."

"I like you stinky."

Jack poked her ribs, looking her up and down and realizing for the first time that she was wearing his shirt. It looked better on her than him ... and it was giving him ideas.

Upon leaving her bedroom he reluctantly climbed back into his boxer shorts but otherwise remained undressed. He was definitely hoping for a repeat after breakfast. Now he wasn't sure they would make it through the meal.

"I see you're wearing my shirt."

"Oh … um … I can change if you want me to," Ivy said, chewing on her lip. "I just … it smelled like you. Wow. That sounded stalker-ish, didn't it?"

Jack grinned. "You can stalk me whenever you want," he said, pulling her in for another hug. He couldn't stop touching her. He didn't think he'd ever want to. "You look good in that shirt. You can't take it off until after we eat. Then I'm going to take it off for you. If you want to smell me, well … ." He involuntarily shuddered when she rubbed her nose against his neck and inhaled deeply. "I'm starting to forget about food again."

"I'm hungry," Ivy admitted. "I haven't really eaten in days. I … can we eat first?"

"Yes," Jack said, loving the giddy bounce to her wagging hips as she rubbed herself against him. "Maybe not if you keep doing that." Jack nipped playfully at her neck, briefly wondering if there was a way to feed and romance her at the same time when the sound of someone clearing their throat in the adjacent living room caught his attention.

Ivy and Jack swiveled in unison, Jack having the foresight to tug Ivy's shirt down so it was covering everything, and found Max standing behind the couch with his keys in hand.

"Does someone want to tell me what's going on here?"

"Good morning, Max," Jack said, tightening his arm around Ivy's waist. "We were just about to make breakfast. Do you want to join us?"

"I'm convinced I'll work up an appetite while beating you to death, so sure," Max deadpanned, his gaze bouncing between his sister and Jack. "How did this happen?"

"How did what happen?" Ivy asked, pasting her best faux innocent look on her face. "I have no idea what you're talking about."

"Oh, cute," Max said. "Someone had better start explaining things to me or I'm going to start yelling."

"You can't yell in my house," Ivy countered. "I'll kick you out. Have you ever considered knocking?"

"See, that's funny," Max shot back. "I let myself in because I was worried when I found out my sister's car was shot off the road yesterday and she ended up in a ditch. I didn't think it was true when I heard the rumor at the diner. I mean, my sister would've called, right?"

Ivy's face fell. "Max, I'm sorry. I kind of … forgot … about that."

"You forgot about getting shot off the road?" Max was incredulous. "Is that because you and Jack clearly made up and … took it to the next level? Because you didn't tell me about that either."

Jack made a face. "I'm really not comfortable with her telling you about that."

"Shut up," Max hissed. "Why didn't anyone call me?"

"I think it's because they were melting down and then making up," Brian said, appearing in the still open doorway and pushing Max out of the way. He scanned Jack and Ivy for a moment and then shook his head. "Yup, pretty much how I pictured it." He shut the door and fixed Max with a harsh look. "There's someone out there trying to hurt your sister. Don't just leave the door open, boy."

Max scowled. "You knew about this? Why didn't you call me?"

"I knew but figured your sister would want to tell you herself," Brian replied calmly. "I didn't realize they would be so caught up in each other they would forget how to use a phone."

"I'm really sorry, Max," Ivy offered lamely. "I honestly did forget."

"That doesn't make me feel any better," Max complained. "I … stop pawing at each other."

Ivy sighed. "Does anyone want breakfast?" She knew there was no way a return to bed with Jack could be negotiated while they had guests.

"Absolutely," Brian said. "While you're cooking, your boyfriend and I need to have a talk."

Ivy blushed at the word "boyfriend," shooting a curious look in Jack's direction. He smiled and offered her a reassuring kiss on the cheek. "That sounds good, doesn't it?"

"Oh, this is going to be an annoying breakfast," Max muttered.

"**THEY** LOOK HAPPY," BRIAN MUSED, SIPPING HIS COFFEE AND watching Jack and Ivy whisper to each other next to the stove.

"They look like they're basking in the afterglow," Max muttered.

Brian shifted his eyes to the only annoyed person in the room. "What's wrong with that?"

"My sister was shot off the road yesterday and today she looks like she doesn't have a care in the world."

"After all those two have been through, I would think you would be happy for them," Brian said. "She's your sister. Don't you want her to be happy?"

"Of course I want her to be happy," Max replied. "I just thought I would get a chance to beat up Jack before they made up."

Brian chuckled. "You're a great athlete, Max, but the only way you'd get the jump on Jack is if he let you."

"Whatever." Max turned his troubled gaze to Ivy, but after a few moments of watching Jack kiss her cheek and pet her head he was done. He couldn't hide the smile. "I'm relieved."

"I am, too," Brian admitted. "I thought they were going to kill each other before they gave in and kissed each other. It will be better now that they're not fighting it ... or each other."

"I have a feeling they're always going to be fighting each other," Max countered. "They get off on it."

"That's the stuff of true love," Brian teased, clearing his throat to draw Jack and Ivy's attention. "I hate to interrupt foreplay hour, but I do have some information."

Jack pressed one more kiss to Ivy's cheek and then took a step away from her. "Did the ballistics match the other shootings?"

"They did," Brian answered. "We found the bullet lodged in the wrecked tire. It's the same gun. I don't think that's a surprise to anyone."

"I'm not very knowledgeable on guns, so forgive me, but wouldn't it be hard to hit a moving tire with a handgun?" Max asked.

Brian shrugged. "Yes and no. Whoever it was probably hid close to the tree line. That's not really very far away from the road. Ivy would've had to be specifically looking for someone to see them."

"What about at the park?"

"That park is open for the most part, but there are still groupings of trees," Brian said. "I'm guessing Ivy and Jack were so wrapped up in each other they didn't pay attention to their surroundings. Once Ivy was shot ... well ... I think Jack had other things on his mind.

"We think we found where the shot was fired from, but there were no shoe prints or anything to help us because of the grass," he continued. "Mark Dalton was shot up close on pavement. We literally don't have anything but the ballistics."

"So where does that leave us?" Ivy asked, doling scrambled eggs and hash browns onto plates and letting Jack deliver them to the table. "What about Marcus Simmons' family? Has anyone been in touch with them?"

"I called his sister yesterday," Jack volunteered. "It was an ... uncomfortable ... conversation, but she said she had no idea that Marcus' gun was even missing. His body was cremated and placed in an urn which Laura says is sitting on her mother's mantle."

"And we're sure that Marcus was the one who died in the accident, right?" Max pressed. "They didn't make a mistake and bury someone else as him, right?"

"We're sure," Jack replied, pulling Ivy's chair out so she could sit before settling next to her. "They ran dental records."

"Did you see the body?"

"Max, I'm eating," Ivy said, making a face.

"I was in the hospital during that time," Jack replied, shifting. He hadn't bothered to put a shirt on because Ivy didn't seem to mind his scars. Now he felt exposed. "I was in and out of consciousness for days, but I have faith that everyone did due diligence on that one."

"So, what are our options?" Max asked, forking a huge mound of hash browns into his mouth. "Did Marcus have a girlfriend?"

"He had about eight different girlfriends," Jack replied. "He fancied himself quite the stud. He didn't spend more than a night or two with any woman."

"He sounds like a real prince," Ivy muttered.

"Oh, don't worry, honey," Jack said, pinching her cheek. "I can't get enough of you."

"Ugh, I'm going to puke," Max grumbled.

"It's nice to see you two getting along," Brian said. "This will make the investigation easier because I was worried Jack was going to implode one of these days while he was thinking about you, Ivy."

Ivy pursed her lips. "I'm glad we're getting along, too."

"The flowers were a nice touch, by the way, Jack," Brian said, chuckling at the adoring way Jack and Ivy looked at each other. "How come you didn't bring them inside, though?"

Jack stilled, dragging his eyes from Ivy's face. "What flowers?"

"The ones out on the side of the porch," Brian said, adding jam to his toast. "They're pretty. I don't understand why you just left them outside, though. I would've thought Ivy would want to put them in a vase. Whenever I buy my wife flowers she talks to them while she arranges them."

"I didn't get Ivy flowers," Jack said, tilting his head to the side. "You saw me walk up the driveway. I didn't have flowers on my mind."

"So who are the flowers from?" Brian asked.

Jack hopped to his feet, cautioning Ivy with a warning finger when she moved to follow him. "You ... keep your head inside. Promise me."

Ivy sighed. "Are we going to start fighting already?"

"Not if you keep your head inside," Jack said, cupping her chin and giving her a quick kiss. "I'll get the flowers."

Brian followed Jack, keeping a wary eye on the surrounding property as Jack grabbed the discarded bouquet and brought it inside. He turned it over, searching it, but they looked like normal flowers.

"Is there a card?" Max asked.

Jack shook his head, his expression distant.

"What is it?" Brian asked.

"These are the same type of flowers ... the exact same mixture ... that I dropped off at Marcus' grave when I got out of the hospital," he said.

"Why would you give the guy who shot you flowers?" Max asked.

"Because I wanted him to know that I won," Jack replied. "I ... it's stupid. I wanted closure."

"You're sure it's the same bouquet?" Brian pressed.

Jack nodded. "I wouldn't forget something like that."

"Well, that's another tie to Marcus," Brian said. "You know what you have to do, right?"

"Yes."

"What do you have to do?" Ivy asked, her voice small.

"I have to go back down to Detroit and talk to Marcus' mother … and some of my old contacts from my days with the department down there," Jack answered.

"But … you're leaving? So soon?" Ivy knew Jack had a job to do, and she couldn't see a way around a trip south either, but the idea of being away from him after just getting him filled her with dread.

"Don't worry, honey," Jack said. "You're going with me."

Ivy brightened. "I am?"

"Of course you are," Jack said. "I just got you. I'm not letting you out of my sight. It will be our first official road trip as a couple. I just hope you're not annoying during a long trip."

Max snorted. "She's annoying no matter what."

Ivy flicked his ear. "You're the one who is annoying."

"Ow!" Max rubbed his ear ruefully and took a step away from Ivy. "What do you want me to do while you guys are out of town?"

Jack arched a challenging eyebrow. "Oh, now you want to help?"

"She is my sister."

"That's good," Jack said, leaning over and scooping Nicodemus up and handing the cat over to Max. "You're going to be needed for babysitting duty. I don't want the cat left alone here while we're gone."

Max scowled. "That doesn't sound like something I can list on my résumé … or use to woo women at the bar."

"I guess you'll just have to use your smile then," Jack said, rolling his eyes. "Come on, honey. You need to finish your breakfast and pack. We have a long drive ahead of us."

"Is it wrong that I'm excited to go out of town with you?"

Jack's expression softened. "If it's wrong, we'll be wrong together."

"Oh, gross," Max said. "You two are definitely going to make me sick."

"Get used to it," Jack shot back. "This is the way it's going to be from now on."

"Just make sure my sister is wearing underwear next time, will you?"

"I can't promise that," Jack said. "I'll do my best, though."

"That's all I ask."

Fifteen

"Well?" Jack cast an expectant look in Ivy's direction, navigating from one freeway to the next and watching her to see how she would react to the city.

"I have been to Detroit before," Ivy said, her gaze trained on the scenery as it flew by. "I'm not some country bumpkin who has never seen asphalt."

Jack pursed his lips. As far as trips went, this one had been pleasant. They talked about everything that crossed their minds, chatting amiably as if they'd known each other for years instead of weeks. They held hands and kissed whenever possible, including whenever there was a break in the traffic or they stopped for a restroom break. Still, the closer they got to the city, the more antsy Ivy got. Jack could read the change in her demeanor no matter what she said. "When was the last time you were down here?"

"Mom and Dad took Max and me to the zoo when I was eight."

Jack chuckled, delighted. "That recently, huh?"

"I know you think I'm a hick when it comes to stuff like this … ."

Jack cut her off. "I didn't say anything of the sort and I certainly don't think that," he scolded. "There's nothing wrong with liking the country. After living in Shadow Lake, I can honestly say I prefer it to the city. I was not making fun of you."

Ivy shifted and met his gaze. "It feels ... oppressive."

"I agree," Jack said, lifting their joined hands and pressing a kiss to Ivy's knuckles. "I had different ideas for our first road trip. You know that, right? This isn't exactly what I had in mind. I just ... there was no way I could be away from you and I had to come down here."

"I know that," Ivy said. "I'm not angry. I'm glad you talked me into bringing regular jeans and T-shirts, though. My skirts would've made me stick out like a sore thumb down here."

"I happen to like your skirts," Jack replied. "I didn't want you to feel out of place down here, though ... well, any more out of place than you obviously do. I promise we'll get through this as quickly as possible."

"Jack, you don't have to entertain me," Ivy chided. "You don't have to make apologies. This is a big deal. This is a big deal for you and for us. This is your first time back and our first trip together. I'm sorry if I gave you the impression I was going to complain."

"This probably makes me a sick man, but I like the way you complain, too," Jack teased. "It makes me smile and turns me on."

"You're definitely a sick man."

"I know."

They rode in comfortable silence for a little bit, Ivy fixated on the increasingly dilapidated buildings and streets. "Where are we?"

"We're crossing into Detroit right now," Jack replied. "This isn't a great area."

"It's kind of sad," Ivy mused. "Look at the houses. I'll bet they were beautiful at one time."

"I'm sure they were," Jack agreed. "This city has been through a lot. There are still pockets where the beauty remains, though. I wouldn't give up on it just yet."

"And where is the zoo?"

Jack barked out a laugh. "That's your only landmark, isn't it?"

"I remember that it was a cool zoo," Ivy explained. "Of course, I've only ever been to two zoos so I didn't have a lot to compare it to. Is it around here?"

"It's actually in Royal Oak," Jack answered. "That's in Oakland County and a much nicer neighborhood."

"Is it wrong that I'm relieved to know that? I don't like the idea of the animals having to hang around in an area like this."

"Nothing you do or say is wrong," Jack said, releasing her hand so he could focus on his driving as the traffic thickened. "I forgot what a pain it was to be down here during rush hour."

"I definitely don't like the traffic."

"You get used to it."

"I wouldn't want to get used to this," Ivy said, wrinkling her nose. "I like wide open places."

"I do, too," Jack agreed. "There's nothing worse than feeling like you can't breathe, and with so many people around down here, that's how I felt a lot of the time."

"How do you feel now?"

Jack smiled. "I feel like I can finally breathe again ... thanks to you."

"That was a really good answer."

"I do my best."

JACK DROVE TO A MIDDLE EASTERN RESTAURANT IN DETROIT'S downtown and parked, taking Ivy's hand and leading her toward the brightly colored building. Her eyes widened when they entered, the kitschy atmosphere causing her to giggle.

"I love this place."

"I thought you would," Jack said, scanning the restaurant for a familiar face. "Have you eaten Middle Eastern food before?"

"I've had vegetarian kebabs."

Jack made a face. "So you've eaten vegetables with a stick through them? You're in for a treat. There's Rick."

Jack led Ivy through the restaurant, not stopping until they were next to a middle-aged man with a bright smile and curious eyes. Jack and Rick greeted each other with a warm handshake and then Jack introduced Ivy. "This is Rick Lawson. We worked together in my Detroit precinct."

"It's nice to meet you," Ivy said, smiling widely and slipping into the booth.

"Well, well, well," Rick said, looking Ivy up and down. "When Jack told me he was moving north I thought it would last three days before he came running back to the city. I see I was wrong on that front."

Ivy was puzzled. "What do you mean?"

"He means that you're pretty, honey," Jack said, rolling his eyes as he reached for the menus. "Don't hit on my woman, Rick. She's got better taste than that."

"Obviously not if she's hanging with the likes of you," Rick teased, although his eyes twinkled as he winked at Ivy. "You look happy."

"I am happy," Jack said, slinging an arm over Ivy's shoulders. "There's a lot on that menu that's vegetarian. Pick a few things to try. We can take the leftovers back to my old house tonight for a snack."

Ivy arched an eyebrow, surprised. "You still have a house down here?" For some reason that knowledge caused her heart to roll. She assumed they would be staying in a hotel.

As if reading her mind, Jack sent her a reassuring squeeze. "I kept the house at first because I didn't know if I would last in Shadow Lake," he admitted. "I put it up on the market almost five weeks ago."

"You did?" Ivy couldn't help but be relieved.

"Exactly twenty-four hours after I met you," Jack confirmed.

Ivy blushed, pleasure warming her. "Oh."

"When did you turn into such a romantic?" Rick asked. "I don't blame you after seeing Ivy, but you've developed a schmaltzy streak."

"She has a way of bringing it out of me," Jack said, smiling as the waitress approached. "Do you know what you want, honey?"

Ivy stilled. Everything on the menu sounded delicious, but she had no way of knowing what to order. "I ... um ... ."

"Do you want me to help you?"

Ivy scowled. "I think I can order food for myself."

Jack ran his tongue over his teeth. "If you order something gross I'm going to make you eat it all and then laugh at you."

Rick chuckled, enjoying their interplay. "While they're duking it out, I'll have the beef kebab with rice and fattoush salad. I'll have whatever is on tap and a glass of water to drink."

The waitress nodded and turned to Jack. "I'll have the same," he said, his eyes trained on Ivy. "She'll have the vegetarian ghallaba with the salad and a glass of red wine. We also want the vegetarian stuffed tomatoes and some hummus."

Ivy's mouth dropped open. "How do you know I'll like that?"

"Because I've seen you eat and I know you'll like it," Jack replied, not missing a beat. "Trust me."

It was a plea more than an order. "Okay," Ivy said, handing the menu to the waitress. "If I don't like it I'm going to punish you later."

"I'm looking forward to it," Jack said, turning his attention back to Rick and finding the older man's shoulders shaking with silent laughter. "What?"

"You two are too cute for words," Rick said. "When did you start eating vegetarian stuff, though?"

"When I started eating her cooking," Jack replied. "She even made me eat crazy mushrooms she picked in a field."

"Those were morels. They're good," Ivy chided.

"They tasted like feet," Jack said. "It's a good thing that she's pretty, because any other man would've run in the other direction when she fed him those mushrooms."

After a few more minutes of light chatter, Jack turned the conversation to more serious matters. "Thanks for meeting me, by the way," he said. "I didn't want to go back to the precinct after everything."

"I understand that," Rick said. "People took sides after what happened with you and Marcus. Dredging all that up in front of an audience wouldn't go over well."

Ivy knit her eyebrows together. "What sides? Marcus shot Jack like a dog in the street and left him for dead."

Jack squeezed Ivy's hand. "Marcus had friends who didn't believe that," he said. "They thought I was making it up."

"Did you make up being shot, too?" Ivy was irate.

"She's a spitfire," Rick said, grinning. "For your information, Ivy, most of the people in that precinct believed Jack. Only one or two of the more ... stubborn ... individuals thought something else was going on."

"I still don't like it," Ivy muttered, crossing her arms over her chest.

"I don't like it either," Rick agreed. "I am curious why you called, though. I'm happy to see you. You look a lot better than you did when you left. I think Ivy here might have a little something to do with that."

"She has everything to do with it," Jack said, causing Ivy to smile again. "We have run into a problem, though." Jack laid out the details of the last few days and when he was done, Rick was flabbergasted.

"How is that even possible?"

"That's a pretty good question," Jack said. "I called Laura Simmons and she thought Marcus' gun burned up when he did."

"I don't know that I've ever asked that specific question, but I think everyone assumed that," Rick said, rubbing his jaw. "I'm just ... I can't believe this. I'm doubly impressed by you, Ivy. It's not every woman who can go from gunshot wound to investigation adventure in the blink of an eye."

"I didn't want to be away from Jack," Ivy admitted.

"There was no way I was letting her out of my sight," Jack added. "Never again." He leaned over and pressed a kiss to Ivy's temple. "I need to know who would care about Marcus enough to go after me. Whoever it is had to have access to his weapon."

"You knew him better than I did."

"It turns out I didn't know him at all," Jack corrected, leaning back as the waitress delivered their appetizers. Conversation ceased until she left, and then Jack lowered his voice. "I'm going to have to go and see his mother and I'm not looking forward to it."

Ivy dished one of the stuffed tomatoes onto her plate and dug in, her eyes lighting up. "Oh, wow."

"I told you," Jack said. "Now you're going to owe me later."

"I'm looking forward to paying up," Ivy said, happily enjoying her food. Jack watched her a moment, amused, and then turned back to Rick. "Has anyone seen Janet since any of this went down?"

"I know a few of the guys went to Marcus' funeral," Rick said, reaching for his own tomato. "Even the ones who knew he was guilty wanted to pay their respects for Janet's sake. I didn't go, but my understanding is that there were fewer than ten people there in total."

"And no one has seen her since?"

Rick shook his head. "I'm sure it was hard for her to come to us and no one knew what to say to her so they stayed away," he said, grinning as he watched ivy enthusiastically dig into the humus. "Don't you ever feed that girl?"

"We've had a long couple of days," Jack said. "She's making up for lost time. How do you think Janet is going to react to me showing up?"

"Well, I think Janet is one of those people who probably thinks her son was framed," Rick answered. "You don't have a choice, though. You have to talk to her. Do you want me to go with you?"

Jack shook his head. "I think it will be better if it's just me." He cast a sidelong look at Ivy. "And my girlfriend, if she's still thin enough to fit through the door, that is."

Ivy frowned. "I heard that."

"There is one thing you should be aware of," Rick said, his tone serious. "After Marcus' death, Janet and Laura filed a lawsuit against the city claiming there was a cover up and Marcus was murdered. Last time I heard it was still winding its way through the courts. She's not liable to be welcoming to you if she really believes what's in that suit."

"Well, like you said, I don't have a choice," Jack said, leaning back as the waitress returned with their entrees.

Ivy's eyes widened as she took in her new offerings. "It's probably good we don't live down here," she said. "I would be as big as a house."

Jack chuckled. "Something tells me I wouldn't be able to stay away from you even if that was the case."

"Something tells me you two are about to go nuclear," Rick said, shaking his head. "Welcome to Detroit, Ivy. I think you're about the best thing that ever happened to this man."

"I know she is," Jack said.

Sixteen

❧

"What's bugging you?" Ivy followed Jack down a quiet street after dinner, their fingers linked, and watched him as his mind worked.

"What?" Jack glanced at Ivy. "Did you say something?"

"I'm trying not to take it personally that you forgot I was even here."

"I could never forget you," Jack replied. "I'm just … something is bugging me."

Ivy waited patiently.

"Laura never mentioned suing the city when we talked," Jack said. "She never said a single thing about it."

"Maybe she didn't feel comfortable talking about it with you," Ivy suggested. "She must feel really … awkward … about what happened. If she doesn't believe her brother is guilty, she might believe you're part of the cover up."

"Laura always struck me as a straight shooter," Jack countered. "She was a little flaky sometimes, but she wasn't the type to lie. If she was uncomfortable with me calling, she would've told me and hung up."

"What do you mean 'she was flaky?' Are you insinuating she was crazy or something?"

Jack chuckled. "No. She was more … bohemian."

Ivy raised a challenging eyebrow. "I'm bohemian. Does that make me flaky?"

"Don't even try to pick a fight," Jack warned. "In general you're one of the least flaky people I know."

"In general? Can you clarify that for my flaky brain?"

"Fine," Jack said, blowing out a frustrated sigh. "If you want to know the truth, you do the occasional flaky thing."

"Like what?"

Jack grinned. He loved it when she got fiery. "Well, for starters, I once watched you tell a cult member that we were out hunting for mushrooms when he caught us spying on him."

"He bought it, didn't he?"

"You locked Kelly in your bedroom and fought off a masked intruder on your own instead of hiding with her," Jack added, referring to a traumatized teen Ivy helped a few weeks before.

"That was a perfectly legitimate reaction to the situation."

Jack rolled his eyes. "How about when you went for a walk in the woods alone one day after being shot?"

Ivy ceased moving forward and pulled her hand away so she could place it on her hip. "I needed time to think. I was upset. You left me in the hospital and I couldn't wrap my head around it. I was gardening but … I had a weird feeling that someone was watching me … so I took a walk. It was a good thing, too, since you were the one watching me."

Jack frowned. "First off, I can never express how sorry I am for walking out of that hospital," he said. "I will beg you to forgive me for the rest of my life if it comes to it. I know what I did was horrible."

Ivy's expression softened. "Jack, I'm sorry. I shouldn't have brought that up."

"You can bring it up whenever you want," Jack said. "I deserve it. Go back to the part about someone watching you garden."

"Not someone. You."

"Honey, I didn't watch you garden that day," Jack said, rolling his neck until it cracked. "I was too upset to go near your house. I was terrified of running into you."

"Then who … ?"

"I don't know," Jack said, hating the fear in her eyes. "Did you actually see someone or just sense them?"

"I just had that feeling you get when you know someone is watching you. I … after I ran into you at the lake, I assumed it was you."

"Why didn't you tell me this when you saw me that day?" Jack was trying really hard to rein in his temper. It wasn't working. "You could've worked it in between the harsh words and the slap."

"You deserved that slap!"

Jack grabbed the front of Ivy's shirt and hauled her to his chest, planting a huge kiss on her lips before separating. "I did deserve that slap. You still should've told me. Someone could've been watching us that entire time."

"I know," Ivy said, her expression rueful as he lowered back to the ground. "I … I forgot about it until just now. I'm sorry."

"Don't be sorry, honey," Jack said. "This is on me. I upset you. I caused you to lose your head."

Despite the seriousness of the situation, Ivy couldn't help but make a face. "Are you suggesting that you caused me to go temporarily insane?"

Jack shot her a charming grin. "I plan on doing it when we get back to my old house tonight, too. I'm just going to use different methods."

They lapsed back into amiable silence, the new information running through Jack's mind as Ivy considered what else she might've missed that day. They reached for each other's hands at the same time, meeting halfway.

"Do you think Laura is capable of killing someone?" Ivy asked after a few moments. "You said she was flaky and bohemian – just like me. That doesn't sound like a killer."

"She's nothing like you," Jack said. "I didn't say you were flaky. I said you occasionally do flaky things."

"That's the same thing," Ivy muttered.

"It's not even remotely the same thing, so stop your pouting," Jack ordered. "You're right, though. The Laura I knew wasn't capable of murdering someone. Whoever walked up to Mark Dalton on the street picked him because he was in close proximity to us. That person looked him in the face before shooting him. They were close. I don't think Laura has that in her."

"Oh, my ... ." Ivy's face drained of color.

"What's wrong?" Jack asked, worried.

"I never put that together," Ivy admitted, her lower lip trembling. "I never even wondered why Mark Dalton was chosen. It's because we were on the street and someone wanted to get your attention because they were watching us and knew you were close. The fact that he was a police officer was just a happy coincidence."

"It's okay, Ivy," Jack said. "None of this is your fault."

"It's not your fault either," Ivy challenged, regaining her senses.

"It's not my fault," Jack conceded. "Mark Dalton would still be alive if it weren't for me, though. That's something I'm going to have to live with."

"Well, by that way of thinking, Mark Dalton would still be alive if you didn't go out of your way to pick a vegetarian restaurant for me," Ivy countered. "He would still be alive if I ate meat."

"Okay, I get what you're saying," Jack said, fighting the urge to roll his eyes. "We could play this game all night. I'm not in the mood, though. I would rather get this really uncomfortable conversation with Janet out of the way and then play another game with you."

A small smile played at the corner of Ivy's lips. "What game is that?"

"Have you ever played naked Twister?"

"No."

"Then you're in for a real treat," Jack said, winking. "Come on. Let's get this over with, shall we? I can think of at least a hundred other things I would rather being doing, and each and every one of them involves you being naked."

"I DON'T THINK ANYONE IS HOME," IVY SAID A FEW MINUTES

later, watching Jack as he shielded his eyes on the front bay window of Janet Simmons' home so he could peer inside. She scuffed at the accumulated newspapers on the front porch. "I'm not sure she's been here in quite some time, in fact."

Jack glanced at Ivy. He had the same feeling. The house looked deserted. "Where would she go?"

"I don't know," Ivy answered. "Maybe she left town because she didn't want everyone staring at her. In a neighborhood like this I'm sure everyone was asking her questions and causing trouble because of what her son did."

"Why would they cause trouble?" Jack asked, extending his hand to take Ivy's and drag her around the side of the house.

"Because most people don't like it when a cop is shot and left for dead," Ivy replied. "She probably got hate mail."

"I think you watch too much television," Jack said, leading Ivy down the side wall of the house, stopping periodically to gaze through windows.

"Are you supposed to be acting like a peeping Tom? It's kind of freaking me out."

"I'm trying to decide if anyone has been here or is coming back," Jack replied, trying the back door to see if it would open. "I need to know where to look next. If Janet has left, we're back to square one."

"Laura didn't mention her mother moving, did she?"

"No. In fact she said that Janet took Marcus' cremains and put them in an urn on her fireplace mantle," Jack said, sheltering his eyes again. "She didn't give a hint that her mother may have moved. I ... ." Jack broke off and narrowed his eyes, gripping Ivy's hand tighter.

"What is it?"

"Honey, I need you to call 911," Jack said quietly.

Ivy's heart sped up, even though she had no idea why. "What?"

"Never mind," Jack said, reaching into his own pocket. "I'll do it. Can you move right over there for me?" He pointed to a spot just off the patio. He was using his patented "cop" voice.

"Jack, what's going on?"

Jack moved with Ivy, keeping a firm hand on her shoulder as he waited for an operator to pick up on the other end. "Yes, I'd like to report a dead body."

"Oh, no."

"HERE WE ARE," JACK SAID WEARILY FOUR HOURS LATER, HIS shoulders slouched as he killed the engine of his truck in front of a nondescript bungalow.

Ivy glanced around the quiet neighborhood. "I don't hear any gunshots."

Jack forced a watery smile for her benefit. "No one will shoot you here. I promise."

Emergency personnel arrived at the Simmons house quickly, declaring Janet Simmons not only dead, but also partially mummified. Ivy wasn't sure what that meant, but she had a feeling Janet was dead on her floor for more than a few days. "Jack … ."

"Let's talk about it tomorrow, honey. There's a lot I need to wrap my mind around, and I'm not ready to do it now. I'm too tired tonight. Is that okay?"

Ivy mutely nodded. Jack hopped out of his truck and moved around to the passenger side to collect Ivy. He grabbed their bags from the back and herded her toward the house. It wasn't until they were already on the other side of the door, Jack engaging three separate locks to keep them safe, that Ivy realized what he was doing.

"Did you just shield me with your body for the walk up the sidewalk?"

Jack stilled. "Not if it's going to cause a fight."

Ivy sighed. "I don't want to fight either. Don't do that again, though."

"No promises," Jack murmured, flipping the hallway light and leading Ivy down to a bare bedroom. There was nothing inside but a bed and dresser.

Ivy looked around blankly and Jack followed her bouncing gaze. "What's wrong?"

"This doesn't feel like a home, Jack," Ivy said, the sparse walls causing her heart to constrict. "No wonder you couldn't breathe here. This place would suffocate anyone."

"I never really thought of it as anything other than a place to sleep when I was done with work every day," Jack admitted, dropping the bags he was carrying on the floor next to the bed. "I never really considered what a home was until I met you. You're my home now."

Ivy's cheeks burned, and when she risked a glance at Jack she almost burst into tears due to the earnest expression on his face. "I really wish you would've gotten your head out of your ass sooner so we didn't miss so much time together."

Jack barked out a laugh. "You're not the only one," he said, opening his arms. "Come on, honey. Let's go to bed. There's nothing left here for us. We'll go home first thing tomorrow."

Ivy stepped into his embrace, resting her head against his chest and snuggling close. "What do you think all of this means, Jack?"

"I don't know."

"Why would someone kill Marcus Simmons' mother?"

"Maybe Marcus had a partner I didn't know about," Jack suggested. "Maybe someone is trying to clean up Marcus' mess. Maybe Janet knew something."

"Like what?"

Jack rubbed the back of Ivy's neck, unconsciously swaying with her in his arms. "Maybe Janet knew what Marcus was up to all along," he said. "Maybe she was involved."

"Or maybe Laura knew."

Jack faltered. He'd been thinking the same thing himself. Ivy's intuition was a marvel. "That could be it, too," he conceded. "I just don't know what to think."

Ivy pulled back so she could meet Jack's somber eyes. "Well, I know one thing we can do," she said.

Jack's expression brightened. "Oh, yeah? What?"

Ivy pointed toward the huge garden tub in the adjoining bathroom. "I've always wanted to take a bath in a Jacuzzi tub."

Jack chuckled. "Well, it seems city life has some merit after all, doesn't it?"

"I don't know," Ivy said. "I'm willing to give it a shot, though."

"Then come on, honey. I'll show you what a real bath looks like."

Seventeen

"We'll be home in about a half hour," Jack said the next afternoon, talking to Brian on his cell phone as he navigated the country road. "Okay. I'll meet you at the station as soon as I get Ivy settled."

Jack disconnected and turned his attention to Ivy. She'd been largely quiet for the duration of their four-hour drive. They slept in as long as they could, the realities of Janet's death and their attempts at a playful bath warring to the point where they were both exhausted.

Rick showed up at the house with the autopsy report shortly before ten, apologizing profusely when he saw Ivy's bedhead – and grim face – and laughing nervously when Jack told him to ignore her because she wasn't a morning person.

They left soon after. There was nothing keeping them in the city.

"Do you want to talk, Ivy?" Jack asked. "I have to go to work for a few hours once I get you home. Now is the time if you want to ask questions."

"I don't know," Ivy admitted. "I'm kind of freaked out by what Rick told us this morning."

"Which part?" Jack asked. "The part where she was shot with the same gun, or the part where the house was so dry she mummified? I'm a little freaked out by that, too. I've heard of it happening, but I never thought I would see it."

"The part where she was dead for at least a month and no one noticed," Ivy said, her voice small.

Jack licked his lips, unsure how to respond. In some ways he felt like he knew Ivy better than he'd ever known anyone. They meshed well together, finding comfort in mutual silence and contemplation. In other ways he was still getting to know her. She was a sensitive soul. Sometimes that sensitivity led to screaming matches. He was fine with that, usually because it led to making up soon after. Right now that sensitivity was making her sad, and he would never be okay with that.

"I don't know what you want me to say," Jack finally admitted. "I want to say the right thing to make you feel better, but I'm not sure what that is."

"Imagine being so alone that no one noticed you died for more than thirty days," Ivy said. "Think about it."

Jack didn't need to think about it. He lived that life for six months after his shooting, opting for isolation instead of engagement because he was wary of people and places. Ivy was the one who drew him out of that world. "It's sad," he acknowledged. "I hope you know that I would figure out you were missing after thirty seconds. That could never happen to you."

Ivy laughed, the sound easing the tension in the vehicle, if only marginally. "I can't believe you would wait thirty seconds."

"I know. It does sound like a lifetime to be away from you."

Jack pulled into Ivy's driveway, killing the engine and pocketing his keys before he could hop out of the truck. He raced around to get to Ivy's door before she could climb out, but she was already halfway there when he appeared in front of her.

"Are you going to shield me with your body again?" Ivy arched a challenging eyebrow.

Jack smirked. "Have you ever considered that I merely enjoy rubbing my body against yours?"

"Of course," Ivy said, nodding. "That's not what you're doing now, though."

"Will you humor me?"

Ivy let loose with a dramatic sigh. "Will you give me a massage when you get back tonight?"

"Can it be a naked massage?"

"Only if you promise to rub me for a full half hour before you try to do something else," Ivy answered.

"I love negotiating with you," Jack said, pressing a sweet kiss to her lips.

Jack didn't relax until they were safely inside and then he set about searching her house. Ivy picked an anxious Nicodemus up and greeted him with a hug as she read Max's note on the counter. Instead of taking Nicodemus to his place – he was convinced the cat would purposely shred his leather couch – Max spent the night at Ivy's.

"Oh, what an idiot," Ivy muttered, making a face at the note.

"What does it say?" Jack asked, returning to the living room.

"It says that Max couldn't sleep in my bed because it has sex cooties so he had to sleep on the couch and Nicodemus tried to smother him while he was out."

Jack laughed at the visual. "Nice."

"He also gave Nicodemus tuna because he didn't like the looks of the dry kibble and now I'm going to have to put up with days of screeching until Nicodemus forgets what tuna tastes like."

"I see who runs this roost," Jack said, stroking Nicodemus' head and kissing Ivy's cheek. "I will see you for dinner. Do you want me to pick up pizza, or do you want to cook something?"

"I can cook."

"How about pizza instead?" Jack suggested.

"Why do you want pizza so badly?"

"Because we can get half of it with meat and half without and our only cleanup will involve throwing the box away," Jack replied. "That will give me more time to focus on your massage."

"You're very pragmatic."

"I do my best," Jack said, smiling. "Is that okay?"

"I suppose," Ivy replied, cozying up to him and rubbing her nose against his chin. "Will you call me if you find anything?"

"Yes," Jack said. "I'll text you dirty suggestions whenever I can to keep you on your toes, too."

"Will you get mushrooms, tomatoes, and onions on my half of the pizza?"

"I won't get onions. I have plans for that mouth and it can't taste like onions."

Ivy narrowed her eyes. "Why don't you get onions, too, and then we'll both stink?"

"Sold," Jack said, kissing her quickly. "Be good and stay out of trouble, okay? If anything happens … ."

"I'll call for my knight in shining armor," Ivy finished.

"You kid, but that's going to be my Halloween costume this year." Jack strode toward the door.

"Really? I'm dressing up like Wonder Woman."

Jack paused with his hand on the knob. "That is why you're my favorite woman in the world," he said. "I know exactly what we're doing for our next dream."

"I'll see you soon," Ivy said.

"I already miss you," Jack replied.

"SHE WAS SHOT TWICE WITH THE SAME GUN?" BRIAN ASKED Jack a half hour later, his face conflicted. "That's not good."

"And she was left on the floor of her house for at least a month without anyone discovering her," Jack supplied. "I don't like what that seems to be pointing toward."

"The daughter. What did you say her name was?"

"Laura Simmons," Jack supplied.

"And I'm guessing that she didn't mention that she hadn't heard from her mother in more than a month," Brian said, pressing the heel of his hand against his forehead. "That does not sound like a good situation."

"It doesn't," Jack agreed.

"You talked to the sister, though, right? She was down in Detroit when you called. That's a lot of driving if she's the one responsible."

"No, my buddy Rick got me her cell phone number," Jack clarified. "I assumed she was in Detroit. I had no reason not to assume that. She could've been anywhere."

"Well, the first thing we have to do is run the cell phone and find out where it has pinged recently," Brian said. "Do you still have the number?"

"It's on the pad on my desk."

"Okay, I'll run that," Brian said. "I was thinking it might be smart for you to start calling around to area hotels and inns. If she's in this area, she has to be staying somewhere. We can run her credit cards while we're at it."

"That's a good idea," Jack said. "At least we have a place to look. If she isn't in the area, the next order of business is calling her again. I don't want to risk that before we know where she's at. I don't want to tip her off."

"Don't you think she's already been informed of her mother's passing?"

"Only if they could find her," Jack replied. "Let's get this moving. I promised Ivy I would bring pizza home for dinner … and then give her a massage without letting my hands wander."

Brian snickered. "Other than the dead body, did you at least get to have a little fun with Ivy?"

"Well, I got to introduce her to Middle Eastern food – which she loved – and a Jacuzzi bath tub – which she really, really loved," Jack said. "What do you think?"

"I think you're a lovesick puppy," Brian replied. "I'd hate to stand in the way of your happiness, though. Let's get cranking."

"WELL, there she is," Michael greeted Ivy with a dark look. "If it isn't my daughter who was shot off the road and didn't bother to tell her parents about it. I can't tell you how wonderful that feels as a parent. If you got a ribbon for it, I would put it right next to the spelling bee one in our photo album."

Ivy scowled as she stared down her father. "It's nice to see you, too, Dad. Say that a little louder. I don't think the people back at the greenhouse heard you."

Michael pursed his lips as he regarded his only daughter. "I am really angry with you."

"Awesome. I'm really angry with you, too."

"What did I do?"

"You're making a scene at my nursery," Ivy answered.

"Fine," Michael grumbled. "How are you feeling?"

Ivy tried to swallow her smile … and failed. "I'm feeling very healthy. Thank you."

Michael pursed his lips. "Your brother told us about walking in on you and Jack naked yesterday morning," he said. "You know very well that's not what I was talking about."

"We were not naked," Ivy shot back, scandalized. "Max is the one who walked into my house without knocking."

"After finding out you were shot off the road and didn't bother to call us," Michael challenged. "I'm usually the one on your side, kid, but not this time."

Ivy tugged on her limited patience and tamped down her sarcastic nature. "I'm sorry I didn't call you," she said. "I really am. Jack and Brian showed up … and there was some yelling and hugging … and then, well, Jack and I decided to work things out."

Michael graced Ivy with the first genuine smile he'd managed to muster since hearing about her accident. "I'm glad you worked things out with Jack," he said. "I'm not surprised, though. No matter what you were screaming to the high heavens, I knew you wouldn't be able to stay away from him."

"How did you know that?"

"Because he's your match, little one," Michael replied, not missing a beat. "No matter how upset your mother makes me … no matter how crazy mad I get … I'll always forgive her and want her in my life. That's how you feel about Jack."

Ivy made a face. "You know we've only known each other for a little more than a month, right?"

"That doesn't matter," Michael said. "When someone is your match, that's it. Jack is your match. I happen to like him and think he's good for you. That being said, next time I see him we're going to have words."

"Dad, I am an adult," Ivy hissed. "I can sleep with whoever I want to sleep with."

Now it was Michael's turn to make a face. "That is not what I was talking about," he said. "I *never* want to talk with Jack about that. I may like to make the occasional joke – mostly because you have prudish tendencies – but I'm still your father and that's icky."

"Icky?"

"Very," Michael said. "I was talking about the fact that he didn't call us after your accident. That should've been the first thing he did."

"Jack was too busy crying after my accident," Ivy admitted. "He was a mess."

Michael's face softened. "Well, everyone is okay," he said. "How was your trip to Detroit?"

Ivy recounted everything for her father, joining in his disgusted reaction to the mummified body, before finishing up with her worries about Jack. "I think he's convinced it's the sister," she said. "I've tried to figure a way around it, but how else does someone not notice when a family member goes missing for a month?"

"Maybe they were on the outs," Michael suggested. "I know it's hard to fathom because our family is so tight, but not everyone gets along like we do."

"Yeah. I guess. Jack said he would call if he gets any news. I'm going to head over and work in the greenhouse if that's okay. I don't feel like dealing with people asking a lot of questions."

"Go nuts," Michael said. "I'm still talking to Jack next time I see him."

"I'm sure he'll be thrilled to verbally spar with you."

Ivy was almost to the greenhouse – and conversational freedom – when a woman cut off her avenue of approach and shot her a nervous smile. "Um … are you a worker here?"

Despite her agitation, Ivy plastered a welcoming expression on her face. "I am. Can I help you?"

"I'm not sure," the woman admitted. "I'm looking for a bush for my mother. She's kind of a homebody and she spends all of her time spying on the neighbors. She thinks they're out to get her. I was kind of hoping you could point me toward a flowering bush that doesn't make too much of a mess so I could plant it in front of her window."

Ivy chuckled. She knew how that went. Her mother was convinced her neighbor was hot for her dad. Ivy was fairly certain that Shirley Deurksen was a lesbian and more interested in Luna than Michael, but she wisely kept that to herself.

"I'm sure I can help you," Ivy said. "Um … ." She broke off, tapping her chin as she thought. "Come on. I think I have something right up your alley."

So much for her afternoon of solitude, Ivy thought as she led the woman toward the far end of the nursery. That was one of the hazards of owning a business, though. The customers always came first.

Eighteen

✦❦✦

"Can you see me?" Rick looked uncomfortable as he stared at his computer screen.

"I can see you," Jack replied, sharing an amused look with Brian. "Can you see me?"

"Yes, you're just as ugly as I remember," Rick muttered. "Put Ivy on. She's pretty to look at."

"Ivy is home resting," Jack said. "She doesn't want to Skype with you."

"I don't want to Skype with me either," Brian said. "It's weird. This is one of those things perverts usually do."

Jack snickered. "This is my partner Brian Nixon," he said by way of introduction. "That's Rick. He's a complainer."

"I don't know why you're so high and mighty," Brian shot back. "You're a complainer, too."

"Isn't that the truth?" Rick lamented. "All I ever heard from him was complaints about the lab taking too long … or the computers breaking down … or a witness lying to him."

Brian smirked. "You're lucky. All I hear about is Ivy Morgan. I've known her since she was a kid. It's a little disconcerting to see him mooning over her the way he is."

Jack scowled. "Can we get back to the topic at hand?"

Brian and Rick ignored him.

"I don't know," Rick said sagely. "I saw her this morning, all cute with her hair standing on end. I can understand why he's mooning over her."

"We all can understand why he's excited to be with her," Brian said. "What we can't understand is why she's lowering her standards to date him."

Jack knew they were teasing, but the words irked him. "She happens to think I'm charming and manly."

"She didn't think you were so charming forty-eight hours ago, did she?"

Jack faltered. "Can we please get back to the situation at hand?"

"He's anxious to get back to Ivy," Brian explained, his eyes twinkling. "He's taking her pizza and giving her a massage."

"Wow. You turned into an over-sharer," Rick mused. "I can't believe I'm actually seeing it."

"It's a Shadow Lake miracle," Brian taunted, causing Jack to growl. "Okay, to the business at hand before Jack blows an artery … did you come up with anything on your end regarding Janet Simmons' death?"

"Yes and no," Rick answered. "We canvassed the neighborhood. The last time anyone saw Janet was at least six weeks ago."

Jack leaned back in his desk chair and rubbed his neck. "Six weeks? What about the smell?"

"That house was locked up tighter than a drum," Rick said. "Someone put plastic wrap under the front and back doors to block drafts."

"Meaning someone knew what they were doing," Brian said.

"I'm not so sure about that," Rick hedged. "The coroner is putting Janet's death around the last few days of May. He says he can't give me a better estimation because he simply doesn't know due to the state of the body.

"This mummification thing is new to all of us," he continued. "The coroner said that whoever put the plastic wrap under the doors and closed up all the windows might not have been planning to mummify Janet. They might have been merely trying to block off the smell."

"That actually makes more sense," Jack said. "The smell should've overpowered the neighborhood given how close the houses over there are. The killer was trying to buy time."

"Well, in buying time, the killer also preserved a lot of evidence," Rick said. "There's fibers and trace evidence on Janet's clothing. The clothing is sort of ... melted ... to her skin, so it's going to take a little time to separate it."

"Thanks for that visual before dinner," Jack said dryly.

"I'm sure once you see Ivy that will fly right out the window," Rick shot back. "Because of the state of the body, if the killer touched Janet, there's a good chance we'll be able to find prints."

"That only helps us if the killer has a record," Brian pointed out.

"Not necessarily," Rick countered. "I think we are all leaning toward Laura for this. It's a sad state of affairs, but there's no reasonable explanation for Laura not to notice her mother was dead for six weeks. If it was Laura, we have her prints on record because she used to work as a volunteer at an area elementary school."

"Unless ... ." Jack broke off, conflicted.

"Unless what?" Brian prodded.

"What if Laura is dead, too? Just because she wasn't at Janet's house and we haven't found a body elsewhere, she could be dead if someone is trying to tie up loose ends in Marcus' world."

"You talked to her, though," Brian pointed out.

"I talked to a woman," Jack clarified. "I'm not sure I can say with any amount of certainty that I was talking to Laura. It's not like I spent a lot of time with her."

"Well, that's an interesting theory," Rick said. "If you didn't talk to Laura, who did you talk to?"

"I have no idea," Jack replied. "No matter how I try to wrap my head around this, I can't see Laura as a killer. If she lost her mind, maybe I can see her taking shots from a distance at Ivy. I don't see her being proficient enough with a handgun to shoot Ivy's tire out, though."

"That's true," Rick said. "I remember her being a bit of a hippie."

"I used the term 'bohemian' with Ivy and she had a fit because she thinks she's bohemian," Jack said.

"Did you kiss and make up?"

Jack scowled. "Don't go there, Rick … and yes."

Rick and Brian exchanged amused smirks.

"Also, I remember Laura and Janet being close," Jack added. "No matter how angry and bent on revenge we want to think Laura is, could she really kill her mother? Could she really walk up to a uniformed police officer on the street and plug him in the chest?"

"That's a good point," Brian said. "Okay, for the sake of argument, let's say Laura is dead. Who would care enough about Marcus to go on a rampage to avenge him? Besides that, why go after you? Marcus is the one who tried to kill you. You didn't do anything to him."

"You said yourself that some people believe Marcus was framed," Jack said. "What if someone thinks I'm the one who framed him?"

"I don't see how that works, but we're obviously dealing with a nut," Rick said. "I still think the easiest answer is Laura. Maybe she took some gun classes. I can check around and see if anyone registered under her name around here. It might take some time, though."

"Let's take this a step further," Brian suggested. "What if we're looking at this the wrong way? What if whoever is going after Jack isn't doing it because they're trying to avenge Marcus' death and restore his honor?"

"Why else would they be doing it?"

"What if Marcus had a partner and they're going after Jack because they believe he ruined whatever side business they had going on?"

"Huh," Rick said, tilting his head to the side as he considered the suggestion. "That's a mighty interesting theory. You know, after Jack was shot and Marcus was laid to rest, a couple of us got together for beers one night. We theorized then that Marcus could have a partner. The problem is, we have no idea who it could be. Other than Jack, Marcus pretty much kept to himself at the department."

"I'm not necessarily suggesting that Marcus' partner was a cop," Brian said. "What if he had a girlfriend?"

"I think I would've known about that," Jack replied. "He liked to boast about his sexual conquests. They were numerous and varied. He didn't like to stick with a woman more than a few nights. In fact, he usually only returned to them if he thought he could talk them into doing something really filthy."

"Oh, well, thanks for that," Brian muttered. "Now I'm going to be wondering what kind of demented things he was doing for the rest of the night. No! Don't tell me. I'm happy living in ignorance."

"If Marcus had a girlfriend, I have no idea who it was," Rick said. "The only person who might know is Laura, and we can't decide if she's a suspect or another victim."

"Maybe I just want to believe she's a victim," Jack mused. "I just can't imagine her killing someone. She never showed any inclination that she could do something like that."

"I agree on that front," Rick said. "This brings me to the really uncomfortable portion of today's festivities, though, and I feel really weird even bringing this up. I think you should have all the information, though, so ... ."

"What?"

"I pulled the files from Marcus' death," Rick said, licking his lips. "I went through everything. One of my biggest problems with this case is the timeline. Jack was shot right around ten at night. Emergency personnel got to him quickly and he named Marcus as his shooter before losing consciousness."

"I remember," Jack said, grimacing. "I thought for sure I was going to die once I closed my eyes."

"Don't get morose," Rick chided. "You didn't die ... and God rewarded you with a hot woman. Do you see how that works?"

Jack rolled his eyes.

"There was nothing out of the ordinary in the file, but something bothered me about it," Rick continued. "I went through the recovered items. There were none. Marcus' wallet burned along with everything else in the car. There was no record of his gun being in the car."

"So, what happened to it?" Brian asked.

"I have no idea," Rick answered. "Police tracked down Marcus on the freeway less than one hour after Jack was shot. Somewhere in that time Marcus made a stop. I think if we find out where, we'll find our culprit."

"He probably dropped the gun off so it could be destroyed," Jack said. "He couldn't be caught with that gun after my death ... and I think he assumed I was already dead when he left. I closed my eyes and held my breath and pretended to be gone."

"That's what kept you alive," Rick said. "There's one other thing ... ."

"What?"

"There's something off about Marcus' autopsy," Rick explained. "I wanted to go through it sheet by sheet in case there was any mention of a gun in his pocket. I thought maybe it got lost at the coroner's office or something."

"Well, don't keep us in suspense," Brian prodded. "What did you find?"

"There's only one signature on Marcus' autopsy when there should be two," Rick replied. "The coroner who signed it was fired about three months ago for stealing from the deceased."

"What do you think that means? It's probably just an oversight."

"I agree," Rick said. "It would be remiss not to at least float the other theory, though."

"What theory is that?"

"The one where maybe Marcus didn't die in that fire and he's still out there," Rick said. "We're trying to track down that coroner, but he's apparently fallen off the face of the earth. What if Marcus didn't die and someone else was in that crash? The coroner easily could've lied in exchange for money. I wouldn't put it past him."

Jack hopped to his feet, his heart pounding. "I ... um ... need to get to Ivy."

"Are we done?" Rick asked.

"I don't like this," Jack said. "I don't want her alone."

"Go," Brian said, waving him off. "We'll catch up tomorrow morning."

Jack nodded. "Yeah ... I ... yeah." Jack strode out of the room without looking back, his mind busy.

Once he was gone, Brian and Rick focused back on each other.

"Do you think he's still alive?" Brian asked.

"Probably not," Rick said. "I didn't want to leave Jack exposed if it's a possibility, though. Marcus would definitely have revenge on his mind. Jack toppled his entire empire. He was selling drugs while working as a police officer. He was apparently making big money."

"Could Marcus kill his own mother?"

"Marcus shot Jack without blinking twice," Rick said. "I think Marcus is capable of almost anything."

"Well, see if you can track down that coroner," Brian instructed. "I'm going to call all of the hotels and inns in this area again and ask about any guests – including males. We've been going on the assumption that this was done by a female for almost a day now. I would hate to think we were wrong."

"There still has to be a woman involved," Rick reminded him. "Jack talked to someone on the phone."

"Maybe he talked to the real Laura and she's involved in this with her brother."

"Maybe," Rick said. "We basically have a whole lot of theories and no facts right now. You keep in touch and I'll do the same. We have to keep Jack safe."

"That won't be easy," Brian said. "He'll die to keep Ivy safe."

"That's the way he's made."

"I THINK YOU'LL BE HAPPY WITH YOUR CHOICE," IVY SAID, smiling at her customer as the woman paid for her new bush with cash. "Hopefully that will cut down on your mother's spying."

"That would be nice," the woman said, bending over so she could lift the plant. "I don't suppose you could help me carry this to my car, could you? It's heavier than I thought."

"Oh, sure."

Ivy moved to help the woman, but her father appeared and nudged her away with his hip.

"Don't even think about it, little missy," Michael chided. "You were told not to lift anything heavy with that shoulder." He shot a bright smile in the customer's direction. "I can carry this for you."

The woman faltered. "Oh, I … she doesn't look hurt."

"Looks can be deceiving," Michael said, hoisting the plant with a grunt and then straightening. "Lead the way and I'll load this up for you. Ivy, if you watch that register for five minutes then I will relieve you of your duties for the day and send you home to your love muffin."

Ivy made a face. "I'm going to let the nickname slide and thank you for the offer," she said. "That sounds like the best news I've heard all day."

Nineteen

"Hello, honey," Ivy said, batting her eyelashes at Jack as he let himself into her house a little after five.

Jack smiled. He couldn't help it. She was the high-point of every good moment he'd experienced since moving to Shadow Lake. He locked the door behind him, double-checking it to make sure, and then carried the pizza box into the kitchen.

After depositing it on the kitchen table, he pulled Ivy into his arms and scorched her with the hottest kiss he could muster.

When they separated, Ivy's eyes widened as she ran a finger over her lips. "That was a really nice greeting."

"That's because the four hours we spent apart felt like four years," Jack said, hoping he sounded boisterous. He didn't want to worry Ivy. He wanted a nice night. He was hoping she wouldn't ask too many questions and force him to ruin things for the two of them.

"Did you get anywhere on the case?"

"Um, we found a few things," Jack said, turning his attention back to the pizza box. "Why don't we use paper plates so we don't have to clean anything up?"

"I can live with that," Ivy said, hopping toward the cupboards and returning with a small stack of plates. "What did you find?"

"I am so hungry I could eat a horse," Jack said, evading the question.

Ivy narrowed her eyes into dangerous slits. She wasn't an idiot. She knew darned well he was hiding something. "Spill, Jack."

"I ... what?"

"Oh, don't flash that cute grin of yours at me and expect me to turn into a puddle of goo and fall at your feet," Ivy scolded. "I know darned well you're hiding something from me. I don't want any secrets between us. I ... please?"

Jack sighed, resigned. "I don't want secrets between us either," he said. "I also want to have a relaxing night, and when I tell you everything I've found today, you're not going to relax."

"I will when you massage me."

"Ugh." Jack made a disgusted sound in the back of his throat.

"Fine," Ivy snapped. "You don't have to touch me."

"Oh, shut up," Jack muttered. "I want to touch you. I want to rub you all over. I just know when I tell you what we found that you're not going to be relaxed, no matter what you say. If you're not relaxed, then I won't be relaxed. I had plans that called for both of us to be relaxed."

Jack sounded like a petulant child and Ivy couldn't stop herself from smiling. "What if I promise that no matter what I'll find a way to relax both of us?"

Jack cocked a challenging eyebrow. "What did you have in mind?"

"Don't worry about it," Ivy said. "Do you think I'm a woman of my word?"

"Yes."

"Then I promise I'll figure something out."

"Fine," Jack said, giving in. "Get your pizza and join me on the couch. This is going to be a long discussion."

"And then a long massage," Ivy reminded him.

"Ivy, nothing in this world could stop me from rubbing you silly tonight," Jack said. "Do you trust me?"

Ivy nodded without hesitation.

"Good," Jack said. "Eat up. We're going to be exhausted by the time we're done with all of this."

"I can live with that."

"HOLY CRAP!" IVY FEARFULLY GLANCED AROUND HER LIVING room. "I ... do you think it's really Marcus?" Despite her promise about relaxing, Ivy quickly turned herself into a ball of nerves when Jack told her about his day. Jack adored everything the woman did, but he really wanted to shake her.

"I don't know," Jack said, wiping the corners of his mouth with a napkin and dropping his empty plate on the pizza box on top of the coffee table. "I don't want to think it's possible, but ... ."

"Oh, Jack," Ivy said, rubbing her thumb against his cheek. "You have to be freaking out."

Jack restlessly grabbed her hand and kissed her greasy fingertips. "I don't know what I am," he said. "I ... eat your dinner, Ivy. You need your strength for relaxing me in a little bit. I don't want you wasting away."

Ivy made a face but did as instructed.

"I'm not sure how I feel about any of this," Jack said. "All the options we have are ... just awful. Say Marcus did survive, where has he been all of this time? What has he been doing? Has he spent the past seven – almost eight – months plotting revenge against me? If so, going after you would be the best way to kill me."

"Jack, it's going to be okay."

"Eat your dinner," Jack repeated. "Laura is another option. I have racked my brain trying to figure out what her endgame could possibly be. She loved her brother. I know she did. Did she love him enough to kill in his memory?"

"I don't ... ."

"Eat."

Ivy rolled her eyes. "You're really bossy tonight." She bit into her pizza and let Jack work out his feelings. She realized he wasn't looking for answers from her. He just wanted someone to talk to. She could definitely be that person.

"You and Max are closer than any brother and sister I've ever seen," Jack said. "I know you love him. I can't see you killing for him, though."

"I might kill him, but no, I wouldn't kill for him."

"Laura was a sweet girl," Jack said. "She was kind ... and she liked to flirt a little bit ... but she was harmless."

Ivy pursed her lips. "She was flirty? Oh, please tell me you didn't sleep with her. I'm going to be so grossed out."

Jack chuckled. "I didn't sleep with her," he said. "She kind of hinted around like she wanted me to ask her out, but I would never do that."

"Because she was flaky?"

"Because I wasn't attracted to her," Jack replied. "You might find this hard to believe, but before you I can't remember the last woman I was genuinely attracted to. They broke the mold with you, honey. I was attracted to you from the moment I saw you and you were rude and mean."

Ivy snorted. "I was not rude and mean," she said. "You treated me like I didn't know what a dead body looked like."

"That's because you were so cute in your little skirt and bare feet," Jack pointed out. "I didn't think anyone that cute could be worldly, too. Imagine my surprise and delight to find out that you were the entire package."

"I'm definitely going to relax your socks off tonight."

Jack grinned, the teasing taking some of the edge off. "Even if I was attracted to her – which I wasn't, so stop making that face – I would never go after a friend's sister. That's just ... tacky."

"You and Max are friends and you went after me."

"Max and I became friends after I was already hopelessly devoted to you," Jack corrected. "There's a difference. I fell for you before I wanted to admit it. I didn't become friendly with Max until I was essentially killing myself because I was trying to stay away from you."

"You're so sweet."

"Besides, I don't know if you've noticed or not, but Max doesn't seem thrilled that we got together," Jack pointed out. "I think he might be rethinking any future friendship."

"You're wrong about Max," Ivy said, finishing her pizza and wiping off her hands before dropping her empty plate on top of Jack's. "Max has been your biggest champion from the beginning. He's just having trouble because he decided to hate you after the hospital incident."

"And rightly so."

"And rightly so," Ivy agreed. "It's hard for him to switch his emotions on and off. He'll be fine in a few days. In the end, he wants me to be happy more than he wants to beat you up."

"And I make you happy, right?"

"Oh, are you fishing for compliments?" Ivy teased.

"I might like a compliment."

"Well, in that case ... yes, you make me very happy."

Jack leaned in and pressed a soft kiss to Ivy's expectant mouth. "You make me happy, too, honey. You make me ... so happy."

"On a side note, though, my father is threatening to have a talk with you because you didn't call him after my accident," Ivy said. "You should probably prepare yourself for that. I tried to talk him out of it, but he wouldn't listen."

"Your father stopped by today? That's nice. He wasn't mad I spirited you out of town, was he?"

"He didn't stop by. I saw him when I was at the nursery. He's fine with the trip. He's just really unhappy about the lack of a phone call."

"What did you just say?"

"My father is going to have a talk with you," Ivy repeated.

"Not that." Jack's mood shifted, anger coursing through him. "What did you say about the nursery?"

Ivy was genuinely confused. "Nothing. I just said I saw my father while I was there today."

"Dammit, Ivy!" Jack roared. "Are you telling me after everything that happened you walked over to that nursery by yourself today?"

Ivy was taken aback. "I ... ."

"Are you trying to kill me?"

Ivy scowled. "Now you listen here, Jack. I'm an adult. That's my business. It's my job to take care of it. I was perfectly safe walking there. It took two minutes."

"You were not perfectly safe," Jack seethed, leaning forward. "What if Marcus was hiding in the woods? What if he shot you? What if he tried to take you?"

"We don't even know if it is Marcus," Ivy pointed out.

"That's not the point!"

"Don't you yell at me," Ivy hissed. "You are not my father. I'm allowed to make decisions regarding my own life. If you don't like that … well … ."

"Well, what?"

Ivy didn't have an answer. There was no way she could even finish the sentence. They both knew what she was going to say before thinking better of it. The problem was, even if she did say the words, both halves of the couple knew it was an empty threat. "Well, nothing."

"Come here," Jack growled, grabbing Ivy's waist and pulling her to a flat position on the couch.

"What are you doing?"

"I'm letting you relax me before I give you a massage," Jack answered. "We both need to relax. Otherwise I'm going to kill you for how stupid you were today."

"Don't call me stupid!"

"Don't do stupid things!"

They reached for each other at the same time, passion exploding as well as pent-up need. As far as relaxation went, there was no better way to get it.

"I THINK WE MIGHT BE SICK IN THE HEAD," IVY SAID AN HOUR later, Jack rubbing the area around her neck as she rested on the floor between his legs.

"Why do you think that?" Jack asked, taking extra care around her shoulder. The last thing he wanted to do was cause her pain. He'd done enough of that for two lifetimes.

"Because we get turned on every time we scream at each other … and we scream at each other a lot. If this keeps up, I'm not going to be able to walk."

Jack chuckled, Ivy's words of wisdom tickling him. "I think we'll figure something out," he said. "You're in shape. You can take it."

"Ha, ha."

"I think we're both a little heightened emotionally right now," Jack said honestly. "Between the shootings … and the possibility of Marcus being alive … and you making me crazy … well, things are bound to get heated."

"I guess."

"I'm sorry I yelled at you," Jack offered. "I didn't mean to frighten you."

"You didn't frighten me," Ivy scoffed. "I know you would never hurt me."

Jack lowered his voice. "I did hurt you, though."

"Not *that* way," Ivy said. "Plus, you know what? I refuse to dwell on that any longer. Brian told me you panicked after the shooting. He told me not to write you off. I didn't want to see it because I was so hurt that it was easier to be angry with you than entertain the idea that you might have a legitimate reason for being a butthead."

"I adore you, Ivy Morgan," Jack said, dropping a kiss on the top of her head.

"I still have twenty minutes of massage in front of me," Ivy reminded him. "Don't even think of stopping. That's the best thing I've felt since … well, the last thing you massaged me with."

"That was just filthy enough to be hot, honey," Jack said, returning to his task. Ivy reached over and snagged the file Jack brought home and started flipping through it. It was full of things regarding Marcus' death.

"The thing is, I know you were hurting more than I was after the shooting," Ivy said. "I saw it on your face in the hospital. I had a tiny wound on my shoulder and you had a gaping one in your heart. It wasn't fair of me to turn on you like I did."

"It was fair, Ivy," Jack countered. "I was being a coward."

"How come you decided to stop being a coward?"

"Because the idea of going another day without touching you was almost enough to kill me," Jack answered. "I don't think you understand how I feel when I'm around you. I'm not sure I understood when I first felt it. I do now, though."

"Try me."

"Oh, now who is fishing for compliments?"

"Come on," Ivy prodded. "I want to hear it. I want to hear all of it whenever you think about stuff like that."

"Okay," Jack acquiesced. "I feel like my skin is on fire every time I touch you. I feel hot ... and not in a sexual way. Although, to be fair, I often feel hot that way, too, when you're around."

Ivy giggled, warming Jack's heart.

"I know this is going to sound crazy, but there are times when I actually feel like my skin is humming when you're around," Jack continued. "My heart feels warm and complete. I can't stop myself from touching you. If I could spend every second of every day for the rest of our lives just holding your hand, I would be a happy man."

"That's going to make the sex pretty boring."

"You're a funny girl, Ivy."

"I do my best," Ivy said, her voice turning serious. "I feel that way, too. Sometimes my fingers itch because they want to touch you. I tried to ignore it ... and then when you kept repeating that you didn't want a relationship, I thought you were taking the decision away from me and I was almost relieved."

"Almost?"

"Part of my heart kept screaming at me that I shouldn't let you walk away," Ivy replied. "I knew I would regret it forever if I lost you."

"Well, you didn't lose me," Jack said, kissing the back of her head. "I won't let us be separated again ... no matter how many boneheaded things you do."

"Me?"

"Okay, both of us," Jack conceded. "I don't want anything but you, Ivy. Please never doubt that."

"That goes double for me."

"Oh, are we turning this into a competition?"

"Yes, and I'm going to win," Ivy said, flipping another page in the file and then stiffening.

"What's wrong?" Jack asked, instantly alert. He could read the change in her body language.

"W-who is this?" Ivy asked, pointing at a photograph of a woman in Marcus' file.

Jack glanced over her shoulder. "That's his sister Laura. She's either dead or somehow involved in all of this."

"She's not dead."

"How do you know?"

"Because she bought a bush at the nursery this afternoon," Ivy admitted. "She tried to get me to help her carry it out to her car and was disappointed when my father stepped in to do the heavy lifting. I ... crap. You were right. I was stupid to go to the nursery."

"Son of a ... !"

Twenty

"Hey, honey," Jack murmured, tightening his arms around Ivy's waist and exhaling heavily the next morning.

Ivy, her mind still cloudy from sleep, shifted her chin so she could study his serene features. "It should be against the law to look as good as you do first thing in the morning."

Jack snickered. "Are you trying to start the morning out on the right foot so we don't fight? If so, that's a nice way to do it."

"If we fight again I definitely won't be able to walk."

Jack stroked the back of Ivy's head and brushed a kiss against her forehead. After the bombshell about Laura stopping by the nursery, he called Brian to see where he was on the hotel search. They were basically at a standstill. With nothing left to do, Jack finished Ivy's massage and then they went to bed – and proceeded to "fight" one more time before falling asleep.

"I don't want to fight with you," Jack said. "Well, at least not right now. You're not the only one who is going to have trouble walking if we keep this up. Don't get me wrong, I actually like fighting with you, but I don't think it's going to get us anywhere right now. I'd rather dole out our fights so we're only doing it once a week or so."

"I need to fight more than once a week. It's what keeps my skin dewy fresh."

Jack snorted. "You really do make me laugh."

Ivy kissed his cheek. "I'm sorry about what happened," she said. "I probably shouldn't have gone to work yesterday. I honestly didn't even think about it."

"Yes, well, we're going to come up with a list of appropriate actions for when your life is in danger. I'm even going to buy one of those fancy chalkboards so I can change it during any given situation."

"Do you foresee my life being in danger a lot?"

"Unfortunately I think danger is attracted to you, honey. I need you to stay alive, so I'm going to have to think outside of the box where you're concerned."

"Do I get to make rules for you on the chalkboard?" Ivy asked.

"Ah, fair is fair, right? I guess so."

"Then the first rule is you can't boss me around," Ivy said. "I'm going to write that one in pink – like my hair – so you don't forget."

"See, now I think you're trying to pick a fight," Jack said. "In the effort to head that off, I have a question for you."

"Okay, shoot."

"Let's not make 'shooting' jokes right now," Jack chided.

"Too soon?"

"Definitely."

"Well, ask your question. I'm dying to hear what it is," Ivy said, her finger lightly tracing one of Jack's scars.

"How come you always push your feet out from under the covers every night?"

Ivy was surprised by the question and glanced down to find both of their feet poking out from beneath the comforter. "I don't know. I guess I don't realize I'm doing it."

"I covered your feet four times last night," Jack said. "Each time you pushed them back out. Do you do that in the winter, too?"

"Yes. Why were you up four times?"

"I like to watch you sleep," Jack replied, not missing a beat. "You're adorable when your mouth is shut."

"Ha, ha," Ivy muttered, although she snuggled a little closer. "If you think it's weird that I push my feet out, why are your feet out, too?"

"My feet got lonely without your feet." He rubbed his left foot against her right for emphasis.

"Okay, that was almost too cute for words," Ivy said, laughing as Jack rolled to his side and kissed her. "Do you have time for breakfast?"

"I'll make time," Jack said, brushing her hair away from her face. "I don't really want to go to work – although that could be said every day when I wake up next to you – but I have to hit the ground running today. Laura is in the area. She's either doing this herself or with someone else. We have to know why."

"The faster we solve the case the faster we can do all the fun things I've been dreaming about since I met you," Ivy said, nipping at his chin.

Jack was intrigued. "What have you been dreaming about doing?"

"I want to go down to the lake on a picnic. I want to go for a hike to my favorite river and hang out – maybe even *fight* out there. I thought we could go horseback riding."

"I like the lake and river ideas. I'm not getting on a horse."

"Why not?"

"They freak me out," Jack admitted. "I always fancied myself a cowboy when I was a kid. Unfortunately, I would've been the only cowboy in the world walking wherever he went. I don't like the idea of being at the mercy of an animal."

"You're at my mercy … and I'm an animal." Ivy mock growled as Jack tickled her ribs.

"We'll definitely go on some picnics together," Jack said, kissing her forehead. "To do that we have to find Laura. So, with that in mind, we need to get out of bed."

Ivy reluctantly rolled away from him, resting her feet on the soft rug beneath her bed and stretching. The movement was enough to have Jack rethinking his decision. Instead, he sucked it up. Once they were free and clear from trouble they could spend as many lazy mornings as they wanted together. He was convinced he would never tire of it.

"What are you doing today?" Jack asked. "If you're going to the nursery, I want to walk you over there myself and talk to your father."

"I'm not going to the nursery today."

Jack was relieved. "Thank you."

"I'm going to Max's lumberyard," Ivy said. "We're supposed to have lunch and I have a few things I need to talk to him about before Aunt Felicity's birthday party. It's in a few weeks. Hey, I'll actually be able to take you as a date. That sounds kind of fun, huh?"

When Ivy turned in Jack's direction she found him leaning forward with an irate look on his face.

"What?"

"You can't go to the lumberyard. That's twenty minutes outside of town."

"I have to go," Ivy said. "I promised."

"No."

"Yes."

"No!"

"Yes!"

Jack lifted the covers.

"What are you doing?" Ivy asked, irritated.

"Get back in here," Jack said. "You're going to kill us both. I hope you're happy. You have no one to blame but yourself when you can't walk in twenty minutes."

Ivy couldn't help but smile. "I'm really starting to like this whole relationship thing."

"YOU LOOK ALL ... GLOWY," MAX SAID TWO HOURS LATER, making a face as Ivy approached him in the sales yard at his lumber business. "How much sex have you been having?"

After graduating from college, Michael and Luna helped Max start his own business – the same as they did with Ivy – and then they sat back and let him sink or swim. Max managed to turn his business into a money making machine, and Ivy was proud of him. That didn't mean he didn't irritate her.

"Don't you think it's a little weird for a brother to ask his sister questions about her sex life?" Ivy challenged.

"I'm not asking you to describe it," Max said, wrinkling his forehead. "Don't ever do that, by the way. What are you doing here?"

"I thought we were having lunch."

"And I thought you were on lockdown until Jack solved the mystery of who was trying to kill you," Max shot back, using a red chalk stick to mark something on the end of a board. "Should you be out without supervision? Heck, how did you even get here? I happen to know your car is still in the garage being fixed from that whole … shooting thing."

Ivy rolled her eyes. "I borrowed Dad's car."

"Does he know?"

"I … yes."

Max narrowed his eyes, suspicious.

"Fine! I waited until he left the front register to help a customer and then I stole his keys," Ivy admitted. "I left him a note."

"How does Jack feel about this?"

"Jack and I came to an … understanding."

"Oh, I can't wait to hear this," Max said. "What understanding?"

"We like to make up after we fight," Ivy answered, not missing a beat. "He likes to yell … and I like to yell … and then we like to make up."

"You two are sick," Max muttered. "How does he really feel? Don't lie to me. I'm not thrilled with Jack right now, but the one thing I can say with absolute certainty is that he would never purposely put your life in danger … that includes letting you do something stupid."

Ivy bit her lip. Max knew her too well. It was annoying. "He walked me over to the nursery, watched me steal Dad's keys, and then threatened me with handcuffs – and not in a fun way – if I wasn't really careful," Ivy explained. "I'm not allowed to drive back to my house. I have to park Dad's car at the nursery and then wait for Jack to walk me back home."

"Oh, it's like a really cute and co-dependent Lifetime movie," Max teased, although his smile told Ivy he was genuinely happy to see her. "I've kind of missed spending time with you over the past few days. I guess now that you and Jack are officially on, I won't be seeing as much of you, huh?"

"We'll still be seeing each other, Max," Ivy countered. "There's no reason to cry. It's just right now … with all that's going on … Jack is kind of glued to my side."

"Don't kid yourself," Max said. "Jack has always wanted to be glued to your side. He finally got his head out of his ass long enough to admit it. This is new. You guys should hopefully calm down once all this blows over. What's going on with the investigation, by the way?"

Ivy related the new developments to Max, sitting at one of the new picnic tables he was offering for sale and resting her chin on her hands. "The thing is, I don't know how to help Jack through this," Ivy admitted when she was done. "What happened to him was tragic and part of me thinks he has to go through whatever he's about to go through alone."

"I think it's sweet that you're putting his feelings ahead of your own," Max said. "That being said, I don't think Jack wants to handle this alone. I think he wants you with him. No matter what happens here, though, it's going to be a blow for Jack. I do think you guys will manage to work it out on your own. You always do."

"I feel like something is off," Ivy admitted.

"What was your first clue? I'm thinking the dead cop, bullet in your shoulder, or being shot off the road should've been it."

"I … if I tell you something, do you promise not to blab it to anyone else? I'm serious."

Max's handsome face sobered. "Okay."

"Aunt Felicity made me do a séance the other day," Ivy said, finally giving voice to something that had been bothering her for days.

"Oh, man, are you kidding me?" Max chuckled. "She tried to do that with me once. Ugh. I remember when you had that sleepover and she tried to do one and you kicked everyone out for making fun of her. Who did she want to talk to? Please tell me it was John Lennon."

"She wanted to contact Marcus Simmons' ghost."

Max stilled. "Seriously? That's … weird and interesting at the same time. Did she get him?"

Ivy furrowed her brow. "Do you believe in stuff like that?"

Max shrugged, noncommittal. "I ... kind of do," he conceded. "Don't you?"

"I ... ." Did she? She couldn't deny she felt something at Felicity's apartment. "If you ever tell anyone I admitted this, I'll sneak into your house and shave your eyebrows. You've been warned."

Max held up his hands, although he couldn't hide his smile. "Lay it on me."

"She was calling to Marcus and yet I felt something," Ivy said, licking her lips. "I felt a presence."

"Are you sure that it wasn't just Aunt Felicity's influence?" Max probed. "She might have convinced you that you were going to feel something so you thought you felt something."

"She didn't feel it, though."

"What exactly did you feel?"

"It wasn't Marcus. I'm sure of that," Ivy said. "It felt female."

"Female? Like ... could you feel boobs?"

Ivy scowled. Leave it to Max to take things to the lowest possible level. "No! You're a pervert!"

"Says the woman having so much sex she forgot to call her brother after she was in an accident," Max muttered.

"The presence just *felt* female," Ivy said. "I didn't hear voices ... or see faces ... or give it much of a chance because I freaked out and ran away. I just ... don't you think that's weird?"

"I think that you're different than I am," Max replied, choosing his words carefully. "You've always felt things in a way that I can't understand. Why do you think you insisted on creating your fairy ring?"

"I ... it's pretty."

"And whenever you're upset that's where you go to think," Max said. "I think that turning your nose up at the possibility of ghosts is pretty funny considering you've been walking in Jack's dreams for weeks."

Ivy rolled her neck. "We're still doing that. I thought maybe after ... you know ... it would stop. If anything it has ramped up. I took him to the ocean for a midnight swim the other night. Last night he took me on a boat ride."

"See, that's amazing to me," Max said. "You guys get to experience everything together."

"You don't think it's weird?"

"Of course it's weird," Max said. "That doesn't mean there's anything wrong with it. I've always thought you had a little bit of magic in you, Ivy. When everyone else was calling you 'weird' and 'dorky' I knew something else was going on. This just proves that."

"You're a good brother." Ivy smiled. "You're a pervert and a pain, but you're still a good brother."

"I know," Max said. "On that note, though, let me go and hand this off to one of my workers and then I'll take you to lunch. I'm dying to hear about your trip to Detroit."

"I tried Middle Eastern food and I got to take a bath in a Jacuzzi tub."

"Oh, well, that sounds fun," Max said. "I'll be back in a minute."

Being alone with her thoughts made Ivy restless. She got to her feet and moved around, studying Max's new summer offerings. The lumberyard offered a bevy of items. Most people who visited were looking for material to finish their do-it-yourself projects. Others liked the homemade picnic tables and swings. In fact, Ivy was considering buying one of the swings herself. She had visions of sitting on the swing with Jack, a blanket, and a glass of wine floating through her head.

Ivy was so lost in thought that she initially ignored the wisp of energy floating in the corner of her eye. After a moment, she waved her hand, thinking it was smoke. She turned, about to unload on someone for the stupidity associated with smoking in a lumberyard when she realized she was looking at something else.

Ivy cocked her head and blinked rapidly, the ethereal figure – more mist than corporeal – mimicked her actions.

"Holy crap," Ivy muttered, staring closer. The figure was so transparent she was having trouble making out facial features. "I … are you really there or am I losing my mind?"

The figure didn't respond. It was definitely female. She could see the telltale edge of a skirt hem just above the figure's knee. "Can you talk?"

"Can you?" Max asked, appearing at Ivy's back.

Ivy jolted, afraid, and when she turned back around the figure was gone. "I ... did you see that?"

"See what?"

"I swear there was something there," Ivy said. "It looked like ... a ghost."

Max laughed. He couldn't help himself. "Have you considered that you think you saw a ghost because we were just talking about ghosts?"

"You said you believed," Ivy protested.

"I do. The timing of this one is a little too coincidental." Max slung an arm over Ivy's shoulders. "Come on. I'll buy you a vegetarian burger down at the log cabin bar on the corner. I think you're acting a little flighty. Maybe you should try eating more and having less sex."

"Oh, puh-leez," Ivy scoffed, casting one more look toward the empty spot where she was sure she saw something. "You would go without food forever if it meant you were having regular sex."

"That is not true," Max countered. "I would miss prime rib too much."

"Well, at least you have your priorities straight."

Twenty-One

"Y ou look better than you did last night," Brian said, his gaze wandering over Jack. "In fact, you look like you had a good night. If I didn't know everything that was going on, I would think you were happy."

"I *am* happy," Jack countered. "I'm also worried."

"How is Ivy?"

Jack made a disgusted sound in the back of his throat. "She's full of herself and a pain in the ass."

"You knew that going in. How is she otherwise? Did she freak out when she realized who she was talking with at the nursery? That had to be scary ... even though she didn't understand what was really happening until after the fact."

"Do you want to know something about Ivy?"

Brian shook his head. "Not if it's dirty," he said. "I still think of her as the eight-year-old girl who brought me a bouquet of flowers when my mother died and told me not to worry because I would see her again. She has a kind heart."

"She does have a kind heart," Jack agreed. "She also only hears what she wants to hear."

Brian barked out a hoarse laugh. "Oh, son, that's not an Ivy thing. That's a woman thing."

"It's annoying," Jack said. "We had a huge fight about her going to that nursery yesterday. I realize now I should've seen it coming, but it never crossed my mind that she would be that stupid."

"You didn't call her stupid, did you?"

Jack shrugged. "Maybe a little."

"Did she make you sleep on the couch?"

"We made up before bed," Jack replied. "She likes to make up as much as she likes to fight." He smiled at the memory.

"And how were things this morning?"

"She does this ridiculously adorable thing where she pokes her feet out of the covers no matter how many times I cover them up during the night."

Brian pursed his lips. "You've got it bad, son. How was she otherwise?"

"Well, she dug her heels in about going to see Max," Jack answered. "I thought I had the upper hand because she doesn't have a car, but then I watched her stroll over to her nursery, schmooze her father, and steal his car when he wasn't looking. She didn't even think twice about it."

Brian laughed. "That sounds about right. Why is she going to see Max?"

"Because she wants me to have a heart attack."

"Why else?"

"Because she wanted to talk to him," Jack said. "She said it was about her aunt's birthday and she promised him lunch, but I think she honestly just wanted to see him."

"Those two are close," Brian said. "You're going to have to get used to that. Ivy didn't have a lot of friends growing up. Max was the opposite. They spent a lot of time together. He always went out of his way to include her ... and protect her when it was necessary. I wouldn't try to get between them."

"I don't want to get between them," Jack argued. "I don't understand why Max couldn't go to her house and see her. I want her to be safe. I don't think I'm being unreasonable."

"Do you want to know what I think?"

"No."

Brian ignored Jack's petulant pout. "I think that you're worked up about this for three reasons," he said. "The first is that you and Ivy finally got together and you can't help yourself from worrying about her. That's normal, especially when things are just getting started. Ivy is an adult, though. She can take care of herself.

"The second reason is that you want to imagine Ivy happy and safe in her home while you're out getting the bad guys," he continued. "That's a man thing. You're going to have to get over that. I did the same thing with my wife and she didn't like it any more than Ivy will. Ivy is a headstrong woman. When it comes down to it, she's going to do what she wants. That's one of the reasons you fell for her. You can't ask her to change to suit your needs now."

Jack rolled his neck until it cracked. "I know I'm being hypocritical."

"The third reason you're so worked up about this is because you think you brought it on her," Brian said, not missing a beat. "Unlike the first two times she almost died, the enemy going after Ivy now is one coming after you. You want to push her away until this is over, but you know that you'll lose any chance of a future with her if you do. Besides that, I don't think your poor heart can take being away from her."

"I don't want to push her away," Jack said. "That's the last thing I want. In fact, if I could spend an entire week locked away with her, I would gladly do it. You're right about me feeling guilty about why this is happening, though. I know it ... and she knows it, too."

"Of course she knows it," Brian scoffed. "She's a smart girl. She also knows that you can't run away from your problems and that you're going to need her when this all comes down.

"You have a choice in front of you, son," he continued. "Do you want to date the woman you fell for, or do you want to try and mold her into something else?"

"Well, when you put it like that ... all I want is Ivy," Jack said. "I don't want her to change. I just wish she would wrap herself in pillows for the next few days and spend her time hiding. I can't help but feel that way."

"Of course you can't," Brian said, turning his attention to his computer when it dinged.

"What is that?" Jack asked, relieved the conversation appeared to be shifting to work rather than his worry over Ivy.

"We have a hit on Laura Simmons," Brian said. "She's registered at the Barker Creek Lodge."

"Where is that?"

"So far out I almost didn't include it in my search," Brian replied. "I think that's what she was hoping for. Come on. I think we're finally getting somewhere."

"THIS PLACE IS NEAT," JACK SAID, LOOKING AROUND THE LOG cabin main office, awestruck. "I mean … look at this place!"

Brian chuckled, crossing his arms over his chest as they waited. After approaching the clerk at the front desk with their request, she nervously said she had to get the owner from the back. They'd been waiting for five minutes. "This is when your city roots come out to play," he said. "Most people in the area know about this place."

"I'm going to bring Ivy here," Jack said. "She would love this place."

"They have dead animal heads on the wall in the dining room."
Jack stilled. "So?"

"So she's a vegetarian and she doesn't like that type of stuff," Brian said. "Think about your audience."

Jack scowled. "I guess you're right," he said. "I just thought it would be cool to rent one of the cabins on the water. She loves nature."

"As long as you get a cabin without animal heads – and you take her to a different spot for dinner – you're probably safe," Brian said. "How was she in Detroit? She's never been what I consider a city girl."

"She was okay," Jack hedged. "I took her to a Middle Eastern restaurant and she loved that. She stuffed her face full of food she's never tried before. I wish there was something comparable around here. I've looked and there isn't.

"She also didn't like the traffic and said she felt smothered," he added.

"She's never going to be comfortable in a city," Brian said. "Are you going to be happy staying in the country?"

"I'm going to be happy wherever she is," Jack said, meaning every word. "I like it here. I never knew it could be this peaceful. I don't want to leave."

"What about your family?"

"I'm sure my mother and sister are plotting to get me to move back south even as we speak," Jack said. "That's not going to happen, though. Even if there was no Ivy ... well ... I could never go back to the city. That's not who I am now."

"That's a good answer," Brian said. "I'm sure Ivy would like reassurance on that front, too. In the back of her mind, she's probably a little concerned."

"Don't worry about that," Jack said. "She was upset when she found out I still had my house down there, but she was thrilled when I told her I put it on the market the day after I met her. I'm pretty sure she knows my intentions."

"Son, she's a woman," Brian countered. "You have to spell those things out for them or they'll make stuff up in their heads. Ivy's a practical woman. She's still got that 'flip yourself out for no reason' gene, because all women do."

"I'll take it under consideration."

Don Lowden, the owner of the Barker Creek Lodge, finally made his way out to the front lobby. He'd clearly been napping when the clerk retrieved him, his watery eyes and confused countenance fooling no one, and he didn't appear thrilled to see Brian and Jack.

"Brian. How is it going?"

"I'm good, Don. How are you?"

"I was taking a nap," Don said. "I guess I'm done with that. I was having a good dream, too. I was on a date with a supermodel. She wanted me to take pictures of her."

"Well, I'm sorry to interrupt that, but we have a situation," Brian said, launching into a redacted tale for Don's benefit. When he was done, he waited to see if the lodge proprietor would give him a hard time about revealing Laura's room.

"I knew there was something fishy about that woman," Don said, rubbing his chin. "She had an air of crazy about her. She reminded me of my first ex-wife. You just know she's the type of woman who will burn all your clothes in a bonfire when you cheat on her."

Jack fought the mad urge to laugh at the statement. "Is she here now?"

"No," Don said. "I saw her drive off about two hours ago."

"How long has she been here?"

"Tonight will be her seventh night," Don replied. "I haven't seen a lot of her. She usually takes off early in the morning and doesn't come back until after dark. A few of our other guests have tried talking to her, but she made a few lewd suggestions to a few of the women and that ended pretty quickly."

Jack knit his eyebrows together. "To the women?"

"Yeah." Don's head bobbed up and down. "I was disappointed, too. She's an attractive woman, but she's only interested in the ladies. I think she's one of them lesbians."

Brian and Jack exchanged an amused look.

"We need to see her room," Brian said. "Can you take us there?"

"You've got it. Anything to get me back to my nap. I'm hoping a nude photo shoot with one of my dream models is in my future."

"DO YOU NEED ME TO STICK AROUND?" DON ASKED A FEW minutes later, pushing Laura's room door open.

"You can go," Brian said. "We might need you to fill out some paperwork later, but I won't know until ... ."

"Holy crap," Jack said, exhaling heavily as he walked into the room. "Will you look at this?"

Brian glanced at the wall Jack was scanning, frowning when he realized what he was looking at. "Yeah, you're definitely going to have to fill out some paperwork, Don."

Curiosity got the better of Don and he followed the two men

inside. "I cannot believe she put push pins in the wall," he complained, scowling. "I'm going to have to get this fixed. Son of a ... ."

"Yeah, that's the real tragedy here," Brian said, cutting him off. "The apparent stalking your guest has been doing is nothing compared to that."

Don wisely left the room after that, and Brian and Jack moved down the bedroom wall gaping at the photos.

Laura had been busy. She'd taken – and printed out – so many photos of Jack and Ivy that they were uncountable. They'd been taken from a distance with a telephoto lens, but there was no mistaking what Laura was doing.

"I don't even know what to say," Jack said, running his finger over Ivy's two-dimensional face in a photo. "I ... ."

"All right, let's take this one step at a time," Brian instructed, trying to get control of the situation. "Can you recognize where any of these photos were taken ... and more importantly, how long ago?"

Jack focused on the first photos. "That was taken the day before our date," he said, pointing. "I stopped in to surprise her at the nursery and took her lunch."

"Okay," Brian said. "We know that she was here at least a full day before she shot Mark Dalton. What else?"

Jack shook his head, his mind overflowing. "That was taken when we arrived at the restaurant for our date." He recognized Ivy's pretty skirt and happy smile. "That was taken when we had our picnic in front of the police station."

"That means she took photos of you before she shot Ivy," Brian said. "That was ballsy in case someone saw her. What else?"

"I'm not sure," Jack said. He moved closer to a photo of Ivy. She was on her knees in her front garden, and when he got a better look at her face he could see her eyes were puffy from crying. "I think this was taken the day after Ivy was shot."

"How can you tell?"

"She's been crying," Jack answered, pained. "She told me she felt someone watching her when she gardened that day. She thought it was me after she found me down by the lake."

"She's not crying now, so don't melt down," Brian instructed. "I'm not sure when this one of Ivy and Max was taken, but it was clearly shot from the woods by Ivy's house. I don't think Max and Ivy have been cavorting like this since Dalton was shot, so that means she might've been in the area even longer than we realize."

"She has," Jack said, his voice dropping. He pointed toward a photograph in the center of everything. "That's Kelly and her brother. That's the night we had a barbecue on the back porch. That was weeks ago."

"So Laura has been watching for a long time," Brian mused. "Why did she wait so long to approach?"

"And I didn't notice any of it."

"You can't be blamed for that," Brian chided. "No one could've expected this. We need to get a team in here to go over this place. We're going to need help from the state."

Jack turned on his heel and stalked toward the door, taking Brian by surprise.

"What are you doing?" Brian asked, following his partner. "We need to go through all of this stuff."

"No, we don't," Jack shot back. "We know what Laura is up to. We know that she wants revenge on me. She's focused that revenge on Ivy. If we want to catch Laura then we have to get to Ivy."

"Don't you understand?" Jack continued. "Laura has been playing with me. She's almost killed Ivy twice. Do you think she's going to miss a third time? I don't. She's readying for her endgame."

"And her endgame is to kill Ivy," Brian said.

"I won't let that happen."

Twenty-Two

After her lunch with Max – and the odd niggling worry that refused to dissipate after seeing the apparition at the lumberyard – Ivy made a decision. She returned her father's car to the nursery, listened to him rail at her about being an irresponsible thief for fifteen minutes straight, and then returned to her cottage.

She was careful during the trek, her eyes wide and her ears alert, but she didn't notice anything out of the ordinary. Once inside she gathered a blanket, bottle of water, and book before leaving again. She locked the house and headed in the direction of her fairy ring. She had a feeling it was the one place that held the answers she needed.

Max was jovial during lunch and the conversation turned to the occult and paranormal. While he was lighthearted regarding the topic, a few of the things he said made sense to Ivy. She was convinced she felt something in Felicity's apartment. She was even more convinced something was trying to make contact with her at Max's lumberyard. If she wanted to know who it was, she was going to have to make things easier on the ghost. What better way than drawing it to a magical place?

It took Ivy about ten minutes to reach her favorite spot in the world. She'd discovered it when she was younger, entranced by the face she swore up and down she could see in the tree. The mushroom circle was another story, and when she did research on the phenomenon she learned about fairy rings.

As a child with few friends and an endless imagination, Ivy was convinced she'd found something that should be coveted. She spent weeks cleaning up the area until she had it exactly how she wanted it. Then she returned to the clearing every day for two weeks, convinced with each visit that she would eventually see something extraordinary.

It never happened ... at least not in the literal sense. The fairy ring had proven to be magical, though. She took Jack there not long after meeting him, and that's where he saved her from a crazy stalker on a dark night a few days later. Given how things were in her life now, Ivy was even more convinced that the fairy ring had power. It led her to Jack – and vice versa – and now it was going to lead her to answers. She had faith.

Upon arriving she spread out her blanket and dropped the bottle of water and book on top of it. She settled in the middle of the mushrooms, glanced at her "tree friend" and closed her eyes. She had no idea what she was doing. Felicity spouted off about yoga and meditating whenever they chatted, enthusiastic about the merits of being in tune with one's soul. Ivy always politely listened – okay, there may have been some eye rolling – and then discarded the information. Sitting still for an hour with only the company of her thoughts never sounded appealing. She was about to change that.

Ivy rested her palms on her knees and closed her eyes, zoning everything out. Then ... she waited. If she thought the ghost would magically appear after five minutes of sitting in the fairy ring, she was about to be sadly disappointed. She was determined to make this work, though. She waited ... and waited ... and waited. Finally, just when she was about to give up, she heard something.

Finally!

JACK WAS ALMOST OUT THE FRONT DOOR OF THE BARKER CREEK Lodge when something occurred to him. He turned quickly, thankful that Don was standing behind the counter and not yet returning to his nap, and moved to the desk.

"You said Laura was saying things to women. What kinds of things?"

"She was just going on and on about how hot they were and how she wanted to spend a night with them," Don replied. "If I didn't know better, I would've thought it was a dude saying it. It must be cool to be a lesbian. You can get away with saying stuff like that and not get punched in the face."

"Yeah," Jack said dryly, making a face. "And you have no idea where she goes every day? Has she ever mentioned Shadow Lake?"

"Not that I can recall. Is Shadow Lake important?"

"It's very important," Jack said. "So is what she's after in Shadow Lake. Brian is staying upstairs until the state police get here. Is there anything else you can remember about Laura?"

"Is Laura that creepy woman who was staying at the end of the hall on the second floor?" the clerk asked.

Jack nodded.

"She didn't say a lot, but she was weird," the clerk said. "She talked to herself sometimes."

"Did you hear anything she said?"

"Not really. Um … she once told herself to shut up. I only know she was talking to herself because there was no one else around."

"So you think she's hearing voices," Jack mused. That would make sense. The Laura he knew was incapable of killing someone. If she had some break with reality, maybe the voices in her head were telling her to get revenge. "Thanks."

"You know she was here a few minutes ago, right?" the clerk called to his back.

Jack swiveled back. "What?"

"After you guys went upstairs she showed up and went up there, too," the clerk volunteered, nervous. "I thought she was going up there because you guys called her or something. She was only up there like thirty seconds before she came running back down and booked outside."

"She knows," Jack said. "She knows we're onto her. There's only one place left for her to go."

Ivy!

"CAN YOU SEE ME?"

Ivy nodded, mesmerized by the figure in front of her. It wasn't solid by any stretch of the imagination, but she could finally make out features. She instantly knew who it was. "You're Laura Simmons."

"How do you know me?" The ghost seemed both relieved and confused.

"Well, we've been looking for you," Ivy said, hoping she didn't sound as panicked as she felt. "We thought you were here hurting people. Um ... I'm a little confused ... if you're a ghost, why were you at my nursery yesterday? Were you a ghost then, too?"

Laura shook her head. "I'm not technically a ghost ... although, well, I don't think I am. Not yet anyway."

"I'm new to all of this, so you're going to have to bear with me," Ivy said, tamping her nervous energy down. "If you're not a ghost, what are you?"

"Lost."

Ivy had so many questions jockeying for top billing in her head she had no idea where to start. "Let's go about this in a rational way and start from the beginning, shall we?"

Laura nodded.

"What happened to you?" That seemed like a safe question.

"I'm not sure," Laura answered. "My mind is muddy about what happened. I remember falling asleep on the couch. I was having an odd dream. My brother was in a car ... he was on the phone and he was swearing up a storm ... and the cops were chasing him."

Ivy's heart rolled. She had a feeling she knew where this story was going. She didn't know how she knew, but she knew. She let Laura continue at her own pace.

"It was weird," Laura said, her face contorting. "It was almost as if I was in his body and seeing things from his perspective. I panicked in the dream and careened over the edge of the expressway guardrail and then … there was some sort of explosion.

"I thought I would wake up on the couch, but when I did wake up I was in the kitchen," she continued. "The funny thing is, even though I was awake, I was convinced I was still asleep. I could feel someone in my head with me, and when I tried to talk, I couldn't make my mouth work. When I tried to walk, I couldn't make my feet work."

"Who was in your head with you?" Ivy already knew the answer.

"It was Marcus," Laura said, confirming Ivy's theory. "He was talking through my mouth. He was as confused as I was at first. He said that he knew he was in trouble and right before the car went out of control he wished he could trade places with someone."

"That sounds like the worst *Freaky Friday* moment ever," Ivy muttered. "Has Marcus been in your body since he died?"

"I wasn't sure he died at that point," Laura admitted. "I knew something happened. I knew it was bad. I knew I hadn't seen him around. Still, through all of that, I thought I was dreaming. That seems pretty stupid now, doesn't it?"

"I don't think it sounds stupid," Ivy countered. "I probably would've jumped to the same conclusion. When did you know differently?"

"Days. Weeks maybe. I'm not sure. Things were really fuzzy. I could hear Marcus. I could think his thoughts … if that makes sense."

Ivy nodded, prodding the woman to continue.

"I know now that Marcus somehow managed to take over my body. I'm still not sure how. I think it might be sheer force of will. He didn't want to die, so he came up with the only solution that not only allowed him to live but also get away with what he did."

"Do you know what he did?"

"I know he shot Jack Harker," Laura replied. "Jack found out that Marcus was running drugs. My brother was skimming whenever they made a drug bust. He always volunteered to inventory everything because that allowed him to fudge the reports."

"Did you know that before he took over your body?"

Laura shook her head. "He would never tell me anything like that," she said. "He knew I would turn him in. I loved my brother. I was aware of his limitations, though. He was a sociopath. I recognized the signs when I was in college. I took a psychology class and I read about it in a book and I realized what he was. Sociopaths can be charming. They can convince you of things. Marcus was a master when it came to that."

"Why didn't you distance yourself from him then?"

"I naively thought I could make things better," Laura said. "I thought maybe he could be saved. It's stupid to think that now, but there it is."

"Could you communicate with Marcus when you were sharing the same body?"

"He could hear me," Laura said. "I would disappear for hours at a time – it was kind of like sleeping without dreams – and I was strongest when I came back. I tried to force him out of me a couple of times, but he threatened to kill my mother if I didn't stop doing it so … I didn't have a choice. I gave in."

Sympathy washed over Ivy. Did Laura know what Marcus did to their mother? "When did you get completely displaced?"

"Several weeks ago," Laura answered. "I'd been spending more and more time out of my body. It was easier that way. Marcus' thoughts were hateful and he kept trying to figure out a way to get revenge on Jack. He blamed him for everything.

"The more time I spent away from my body the harder it was to return," she continued. "The final straw was when Marcus went out to an empty field in Detroit. I think it used to be an apartment building, but it was torn down. He dug up the gun he used to shoot Jack, all the time mumbling about how he was going to make him pay. I didn't want to deal with him one second longer than I had to."

The next question was a hard one, but Ivy had to ask it. "Do you know what Marcus did to your mother?"

Laura nodded, her green eyes sad. "I didn't know when he did it. I wasn't there. I think he knew that. He told me after the fact that Mom figured out what was going on. I still don't know how. If anyone could recognize Marcus' putrid soul, though, it was her. She knew what he was long before I did."

"And yet she protected him," Ivy pointed out. "Why did she do that?"

"He was her son. She wasn't the type of woman who could turn her back on her own flesh and blood."

"So Marcus killed your mother because she figured things out," Ivy said. "You were growing weaker and weaker ... which let Marcus get stronger. He spent six months thinking up revenge schemes before deciding to go after Jack. I wonder why he waited for so long."

"I can't answer that," Laura said. "It used to be that I popped out of existence when I went to ... sleep. I made a conscious decision to leave my body at some point. That's when I started existing outside of it, too. I still disappear sometimes, but when I'm here I can control my actions. I can go places."

"Did you follow Marcus up here for a reason?"

"I'm still hoping to get my body back," Laura admitted. "It seems ridiculous to say it, but that's all I have. I'm nothing here."

"You know if you do get it back that you're going to be arrested and charged with the murder of a police officer, right?" Ivy asked. "I don't know any judge who is going to believe you were possessed by your murderous brother's spirit."

"I know," Laura said. "I simply don't know what else to do."

"Marcus has been watching us for days, hasn't he?"

"Try weeks."

Ivy frowned. That was disconcerting. "Why didn't he kill me that day in the park?"

"I don't know," Laura replied. "I've been watching him. I've tried to hijack my body back a few times, but he's stronger than I am and he screams at me to get out. I can't seem to break through. If I had to guess, though, I would say he's playing with Jack. He wants Jack to be terrified about potentially losing you ... he wants to toy with him ... and then he's going to kill you."

"What does he hope to accomplish by doing that?"

"He only cares that he causes Jack pain," Laura said. "If you want to know the truth, I think Marcus' biggest problem is that Jack was too stubborn to die on that street. Marcus wanted Jack dead because he ruined his side business. Jack surviving proved Marcus wasn't as strong as he thought. Jack was stronger."

"Jack is the strongest person I know," Ivy said. "Does Marcus want to kill Jack, too? Will he settle for killing me and leaving Jack to mourn?"

"No. He wants Jack dead, too. He just wants him to suffer a lot before he finally kills him. Mark my words, when Marcus does finally go after Jack, he's going to torture him for days first. It won't be a quick death."

Ivy swallowed the lump in her throat. "Where is Marcus now?"

"He's coming for you."

"IVY!"

Jack was enraged by the time he walked through Ivy's front door. After calling Max and finding out she was already gone, and stopping by the nursery to have Michael tell him she returned home, Jack was beside himself. To top it all off, she wasn't answering her phone.

The cottage appeared empty, which didn't make any sense. Michael had his car back. Ivy had no means of transportation other than her feet. Where would she go?

"Ivy!"

Nothing.

Jack turned when he heard shuffling in the doorway, a bellow ready to escape his mouth when he saw her. He wanted to shake her for scaring him like this.

"You are in so much trouble you're not going to be able to walk for days," Jack hissed, swiveling. His eyes widened when he caught of Laura Simmons standing behind him.

"That's not a very nice thing to say to a lady," Laura said, her green eyes shifting brown momentarily before she slammed the vase from Ivy's front table against the side of his head.

Jack saw the blow coming, but it was too late to stop it. He staggered and fell, falling forward. His last thought was of Ivy. He was convinced he would never see her again.

Twenty-Three

I vy found her front door open when she returned to the house, Laura drifting along beside her. Outside of the fairy ring Ivy was having a harder time seeing the morose ghost. She could hear her, though, and Ivy considered that a win ... for now.

"Let me go in first," Laura hissed. "I'll know if he's in there."

Ivy bit her lip and nodded. She had to be smart about this, if only for Jack's sake. It took Laura what seemed like forever to search the cottage. When she returned, Ivy felt her rather than saw her.

"The house is empty, but it looks like something happened inside," Laura said.

Ivy pushed her way into the cottage, frowning when she saw the remnants of the shattered vase. She knelt, picking up a few shards to study them. There was blood on one of the pieces.

"Someone has been hurt," Ivy said, biting her lip. "I ... Nicodemus!"

The cat was the first thing that popped into her mind. She'd found him in a Dumpster, near death, and bottle-fed him back to health. She loved him as much as was humanly possible. If Marcus didn't have any qualms about shooting an innocent police officer in the middle of the street, she knew killing Nicodemus would be easy.

"Nicodemus!" Ivy raced down the hallway, throwing open her bedroom door and found the cat lazily cleaning himself on her bed. She cried out in relief, gathering him in her arms and hugging him. He didn't like being crowded, so he batted her face away when she tried to kiss him and wriggled out of her arms. He was safe. That was all that mattered.

Ivy returned to the living room, studying the floor with a mixture of dread and curiosity. "Maybe I should call my dad," she said, glancing around. She'd left her cell phone to charge on the table behind the couch. It was still there. "He was working over at the nursery. He might've come over here if he was hungry or wanted to check on me."

"Something bad happened here," Laura said. "I think it was Marcus."

"I'm betting money it was Marcus," Ivy said, touching her phone screen and sighing when she saw three missed calls. All of them were from Jack. "God, I hope Marcus doesn't have my dad." Ivy was worried for an entirely different reason this time. She punched up her voicemail button and pressed the phone to her ear. "I'll bet Jack panicked when he couldn't get me on the phone and sent my dad over here to check on me. Oh, God!"

Ivy listened to Jack's increasingly frantic voicemails back-to-back-to-back and then dialed her father's number. He picked up on the second ring.

"What do you want, car thief?"

"Thank God," Ivy cried out, relief washing over her. "I thought something happened to you."

"Why would you think that?" Michael asked.

"I just got back from my fairy ring and the front door was open," Ivy explained. "The vase I had by the door is smashed on the floor and I'm sure there's blood on it. I thought maybe Nicodemus was hurt at first, but I found him and he's fine. My next thought was of you."

"Ivy, have you tried calling Jack?"

"No. I had three voicemails from him, though. I left the phone in the house to charge while I was at my fairy ring. Why? Is he mad?"

"They found Laura Simmons' hotel room," Michael said. "Jack

called me about ... I don't know ... forty-five minutes ago. She's been stalking you. She had hundreds of photos of you and Jack.

"Jack thinks she's coming for you right now," Michael continued. "He was on his way to your house."

Ivy's heart rolled. "No ... ."

"Is his truck there?"

Ivy glanced out at the driveway. She would've noticed Jack's truck on approach. It wasn't there. "No. He's not here."

"That doesn't mean he wasn't there," Michael said. "You hang up and lock the door. Call Brian and tell him what's going on. I'll be there in two minutes. Don't open that door for anyone but me. Do you understand?"

Ivy nodded, tears filling her eyes. "Dad ... ."

"We'll find Jack," Michael said. "We'll find him."

JACK WOKE IN A DARK ROOM, HIS HEAD THROBBING. HE TRIED to focus, but the edges of his eyesight were blurry. He probably had a concussion. He tried to remember the last thing that happened, and that's when Laura's smiling face swam into view.

He moved quickly, trying to push himself up from the chair he sat in, only to find himself tied in place, his hands secured behind him. He swore, tilting his head to the side and listening. There it was. Someone was in the room with him. He could hear breathing.

"Laura?"

A light snapped on, causing Jack to close his eyes to ward off the glare. When he risked opening them again, it took a moment for his eyes to adjust. He was in a basement, the only light coming from a naked bulb with a chain overhead.

Laura stood beneath the light. She was dressed in jeans and a T-shirt, her hair pulled back in a ponytail and her face bare of makeup. She looked like a different person.

"Where are we?" Jack asked.

"In a safe place," Laura replied. "I've been scouting locations for a week. This house is empty because the owners moved to Bay City. I set up a showing with a local realtor and got the combination for the lockbox on the door. It was pretty easy to gain access. The place is ours ... and there are no neighbors within screaming distance."

Laura looked pleased with herself.

"Where is Ivy?"

"Oh, little Miss Ivy evaded me," Laura said, rolling her eyes. "I was trying to get her, but she disappeared into the woods. I was following her, but I somehow lost her. I gave up and went back to her cottage to wait for her to return – I was going to kill her there and leave you to find her dead in her bed with a bunch of roses spread around her – but you showed up instead.

"I had to make a choice," she continued. "I knew I was running out of time after seeing you at the hotel. As much as I want Ivy, I want you more. I had to settle for you. I guess Ivy gets a pass ... for now."

Despite his predicament, Jack was secretly relieved. Ivy was safe. With his disappearance, Brian, Max, and Michael would rally around her. She wouldn't be alone. If the unthinkable happened and Laura managed to kill him, at least he would pass with the knowledge that Ivy would live on. That was everything to him.

"I don't understand why you're doing this, Laura," Jack said, deciding to approach the woman from a place of friendship and shared mutual pain. "I know you loved your brother, but is this really what you want to do?"

Laura contorted her face in dramatic fashion. "You still don't get it, do you?"

"Get what?"

"I'm not Laura. I'm Marcus."

Jack bit the inside of his cheek, unsure. Was Laura so mentally unbalanced she thought she was Marcus? That was a problem he wasn't expecting. "You're not Marcus. You're Laura Simmons. Marcus was your brother. Deep down inside, you have to know that."

"You're such an ass," Laura said. "I know who I am. I'm Marcus. Somehow I managed to jump out of my body right before I flew over that guardrail. I landed in Laura's body. She was asleep, so it was pretty easy for me to push her out."

That was the most ludicrous thing Jack had ever heard. "Did you see that on a television show or something?"

Laura frowned. "Do you really not believe me? Are you going to force me to prove myself to you?"

Jack considered the question. Maybe there was hope for Laura if he proved that Marcus wasn't inside of her. Maybe she would finally see the truth of what she'd done if he could somehow manage that. "Let's do that," he suggested. "Prove to me you're Marcus."

"Okay." Laura tapped her lip as she thought, eerily mimicking one of her brother's mannerisms perfectly. Jack swallowed hard. She was really going all out. "Okay," Laura said, taking a step forward. "Six months after we became partners we went out for our first beer together. It was a little Irish pub on the south side of the Cass Corridor.

"I bet you that I could pick up a girl before you could," Laura continued. "We made an agreement about overtime and I approached a brunette with huge boobs. You went after a mousy thing at the bar. She shot you down and I went home with the brunette."

Jack's heart rate sped up. That was true. He remembered that night. Still ... . "Marcus could've told you that story," he said, choosing his words carefully. "He liked to boast about his sexual prowess. I'm not sure why he would do that with his sister, but I wouldn't put it past him."

"Oh, good grief!" Laura kicked an empty bucket across the basement, the sound echoing throughout the space. "Fine. If you don't believe me, ask me something that only Marcus would know. Make it as obscure as you want."

"Okay." Jack licked his lips. "What happened to the gun Marcus used to shoot me with? How did you get it?"

"That's not the type of question I was talking about," Laura snapped. "I'll answer it for you because I know how you like answers, but then you're going to ask me another question. After I shot you – and I was sure you were dead, so I have no idea how you managed to survive – I knew I had to get rid of the gun.

"I drove to that old lot where we used to question narcs and dug a hole and buried it," she continued. "I dug it up again about six weeks ago and used it on my mother because she would not shut her filthy hole. She figured out that I switched places with Laura and she was threatening to do an exorcism on me. The old bat always was a super-stitious moron."

Jack shook his head. "But … ."

"No! Ask me something to prove that I'm Marcus," Laura instructed. "This isn't going to be any fun if you don't believe."

"Fine," Jack said, searching his memory. "Um … what did I tell you after the prostitute murder at the Renaissance Center? We were in the elevator on our way down, and I confided something in you. What was it?"

Laura screwed up her face in concentration. Jack was convinced he'd won until her eyes brightened. "You told me that you didn't understand how anyone could hire a professional because sex was so much better when emotions were involved," she said, chortling. "You said you believed you would find love one day. I guess you did, huh?"

Jack was dumbfounded. There was no way Laura could know anything about that conversation, and there was no reason for Marcus to ever confide anything of the sort in his sister. "Marcus?"

"There it is," Marcus said, gleefully bending over to stare Jack in the eye on an even level. "How's it going, buddy?"

"I DON'T KNOW WHAT TO DO," IVY SAID, PACING HER LIVING room as Brian and Michael watched. "He's out there somewhere. Marcus is going to torture him to death. We have to do something."

Brian rubbed the back of his neck, conflicted. He was convinced Ivy was losing her mind. "Sweetie, I think you're in shock," he said. "Marcus Simmons is dead. Laura is the one behind all of this."

Ivy rolled her eyes. "I can't explain this to you right now," she said. "I know that Laura Simmons' body is doing all these things. Marcus is inside of her, though. We're not going to find Jack by thinking like Laura would. We have to think like Marcus would."

Speaking of Laura, Ivy hadn't heard a peep from the ghost since her father arrived. She wanted to talk to her. She wanted to ask a thousand different questions, and yet she knew if she started holding a conversation with thin air Brian and Michael would have her committed.

"Honey, why do you think that?" Michael asked, his voice soft. "Did you hit your head?"

Ivy slapped his hand away when he tried to rub it down the back of her head. "No!"

"I can't deal with this right now," Brian said, exchanging a worried look with Michael. "Jack is out there. A crazy woman bent on revenge has him somewhere. We found Laura's car abandoned on the side of the road about a mile down. That means she has Jack's truck. That's why Ivy didn't see it when she returned to the house."

"How are you going to find Jack?" Michael asked.

"The state police are sending everything they've got," Brian answered. "Bellaire is, too. They want Laura badly because she took out one of their own. We're setting up a search grid and going from there." He darted a look in Ivy's direction. "Ivy, you need to stay here with your father. I'll call as soon as we know something."

Ivy made a face and turned away from Brian and her father. She knew they were trying to do the right thing by her, but she was frustrated. She couldn't listen to them when she had to focus on Jack. He needed her. Somehow, deep inside, she knew she would have to be the one to save him.

"I'm going to lay down," Ivy announced, moving toward the hallway. "I feel sick to my stomach and my head is pounding. I … need to lay down."

"I think that's a good idea," Michael said, his heart breaking for his only daughter. If Jack died, he knew Ivy would never recover. He had no idea how to console her, though. "Do you want me to bring you anything?"

"I just want to be alone," Ivy said, fighting back tears. "Just … leave me alone."

She stalked into her bedroom and slammed the door shut with enough force to scare Nicodemus off the bed. He shot her a disdainful look before crawling under it. He was not having a good day.

"Laura?" Ivy hissed, keeping her voice low. "Are you here?"

"I'm here. I'm sorry I didn't say anything. I didn't want to risk them thinking you were crazy."

"They already think I'm crazy," Ivy grumbled. "Where would Marcus take Jack?"

"I can't be sure, but he went and looked at an empty house about a week ago," Laura said. "I've been racking my brain, and I think that's where he took him. He would need privacy to do what he wants to do, and that's the best place to get it. The house was in the middle of nowhere."

"Do you think you could find it again?"

"Yes."

Ivy moved to her dresser and opened the top drawer, digging around in the dark until she found what she was looking for.

"Are those keys?" Laura asked. "What are they for?"

"My father's car," Ivy replied. "I forgot I even had them until he went off about me stealing his car this afternoon."

"What are you going to do with them?"

"We're going to wait for Brian to leave so he doesn't catch us and then I'm going to climb out the window and go to the nursery and steal my father's car again."

"What if he hears you?"

"The car is across the way at the nursery. He ran here to get to me. He won't hear it." Ivy was grim. "Then you're going to lead me to Jack. Once we're sure he's there, I'll call Brian with the location."

"Are you sure you want to do this?"

"I'm sure I can't lose Jack," Ivy replied. "I'd rather die with him than live without him."

Twenty-Four

✦✦✦

"I don't understand," Jack said, his mouth dry. "How is this possible?"

"You're asking the wrong person," Marcus said. "I didn't even believe in this stuff until it happened. The last thing I remember is wishing I could be in someone else's body and then … poof … I was. I woke up on Laura's couch and went into the bathroom, thinking I somehow must've passed out at her house or I was dreaming, and then I realized what happened."

"But … that's insane."

"I'm right there with you, buddy," Marcus said, laughing maniacally. "It took me a week to realize it was really happening. After that I started planning my revenge. Do you know how surreal it was to go to my own funeral in my sister's body? Creepy.

"I couldn't take a shower for a week because the idea of seeing Laura's naked body was so gross," he continued. "I smelled so bad my mother finally insisted I reintroduce myself to soap. She assumed poor Laura was grieving."

"What happened to Laura?"

"She hung around in my new brain with me for a little bit," Marcus replied, his eyes flashing with annoyance. "She kept nattering on and on about me leaving because that was my only true escape. I kept telling her to shut up ... and then she would go away for days sometimes and I thought I'd won ... but every time she came back begging me to do the right thing. She always was a moron."

Jack couldn't decide if he was lost in a nightmare or if this was really happening. If this was a nightmare, his only hope was Ivy finding him to drag him away. Maybe he was still unconscious. That was a more reasonable assumption than believing Marcus somehow managed to body jump.

"Where is Laura now?"

"She left," Marcus replied. "She was there when I dug up the gun and she called me a bad man." His tone was mocking. "She said that karma was going to get me no matter what. I knew that wasn't true. If karma was going to get me I would've died on the expressway that night."

"You did die that night," Jack said, his voice wavering.

"Nope. Now I get to finish what I started. I'm going to kill you, Jack. I'm going to make it hurt, too. When I'm done, I'm going to find a way to get your precious Ivy. I'll send her along to the other side soon after I'm done with you. Your biggest problem is that I want to take my time. You're going to have to do some suffering before I let you die. I hope you're ready for it."

Jack's heart thudded at the thought of Marcus putting his hands on Ivy. "Leave Ivy alone."

"Is that all you care about? What about you? Don't you want to beg for your life?"

"I'll beg for Ivy's life if it makes a difference," Jack offered. "I won't beg for myself."

"Have it your way," Marcus said. "Ivy is dying, though. I'll just bet they bury you guys next to each other. It will be sweet and romantic. I can't wait to see how she screams."

"WELL?" LAURA ASKED, HER VOICE CLOSE TO IVY'S EAR.

"You were right," Ivy whispered. She stepped away from the half-window of the old Winchester house and dug her phone out of her pocket. "Keep watching them. I have to make a call … and then we're going in."

"What are you going to do when we get inside?"

"Save Jack … and hopefully figure out a way for you to get your body back." Ivy pressed the phone to her ear and waited for Brian to pick up. When he did, he sounded irritated. Ivy cut him off before he could get a full head of steam. "I know you think I'm crazy, and I don't blame you. I'm not at my house, though."

"Where are you?"

"I crawled out the window and stole my father's car," Ivy replied, her voice even. "He's probably panicking right now, but I had to find Jack. He's at the old Winchester house on Cedar Creek Road. Do you know where that is?"

Brian was flabbergasted. "How did you find him?"

"You won't believe me if I tell you," Ivy answered. "He's in the basement and he's tied to a chair. I'm going in after him."

"Don't you even think about it!" Brian roared. "The one thing in this world Jack wants above everything else is for you to be safe. If you go into that house, you'll both be in danger."

"If I don't go into that house, Laura is going to torture Jack to death," Ivy countered. "You're on your way. I can distract her until you get here."

"No!"

"I'm hanging up my phone now," Ivy said, eerily calm. "I'm going into that basement. I'm going to save Jack. I'm going to need you to save me. I'm turning off my phone so it doesn't give me away. I … if something happens, tell my father I'm sorry. I can't leave Jack, though."

Ivy cut off Brian's colorful swearing and disconnected her phone, powering it off before Brian could call back. She pocketed the device and squared her shoulders before moving toward the front door. "I'm coming, Jack."

"I WON'T LET YOU HURT IVY," JACK SAID, GLANCING AROUND the basement for a hint of something he could use as a weapon. He had no idea how he was going to get out of his bonds, but he'd been shifting his wrists and managed to loosen them, although only marginally.

"What is it about that chick?" Marcus asked, twirling around the floor-to-ceiling beam. "I mean, she's hot. I can see that. You're hopelessly in love with her, though. I can't remember ever seeing you like this with a woman."

"Ivy isn't like any other woman in the world."

"Is it the pink hair? Is that what does it for you?"

"The whole package does it for me," Jack replied. "You need to stay away from her."

"Oh, we both know I can't do that, Jack," Marcus said. "You ruined my life and I'm going to ruin yours. The truly sad part is that you won't be alive to see Ivy die. Maybe I can keep you alive long enough to figure out a way to get her, too. I would love to watch you try to save her. That's my idea of fun."

"I will kill you," Jack seethed, yanking against the ropes as he tried to throw himself forward. "Don't you even think about touching her!"

"I'm going to touch her, Jack," Marcus said, grinning. "I'm going to touch her in every way possible. Granted, it won't be as much fun as a woman, but I'm sure I can figure something out to give us both a thrill."

"That sounds fairly disgusting," Ivy said, appearing at the bottom of the stairs.

Marcus jumped at the sight of her, flustered, while Jack's heart rolled.

"Get out of here, Ivy!" Jack screamed. "Run!"

Ivy ignored his outburst. "How's it going, Marcus?"

Marcus stilled. "What did you just call me?"

"Marcus."

"How did you know that?"

"Well, I spent the afternoon with your sister," Ivy replied, keeping her hand on the stair railing and her eyes on Marcus. She wanted to reassure Jack that help was coming, but tipping off Marcus didn't seem like a good idea. "She's approached me a few times. Today we finally got to have a chat."

Marcus narrowed his eyes. "How is that even possible?"

"How is it possible that you're inside of her body?"

"I have no idea," Marcus answered. "Does she know? Has she figured it out?"

Ivy pursed her lips. "She's figured out a few things," she conceded. "She knows you killed your mother. She knows you killed Mark Dalton. She figured out what you had planned for Jack and me. She's the one who told me about this place. She's been following you."

Marcus glanced around the basement, narrowing his eyes. "Is she here now?"

"She is."

"Why can't I see her?"

"I can't see her either," Ivy admitted. "I saw her briefly this afternoon, but I can hear her. She's been bending my ear a lot today. It seems you've been a very bad boy."

"Ivy, if you don't run, I'm never going to forgive you," Jack ordered. "You have to get out of here, honey. Please."

"I'm not leaving you, Jack. Stop telling me to leave you. It's not going to happen."

"Yeah, Jack. Shut up," Marcus said, mocking him. "If Laura is still here, what is she doing?"

"She's waiting for the perfect time to get her body back," Ivy replied. "She knows you're too powerful to wrest control away from you. She needs to sneak back in when you're not in control … like maybe if you were unconscious or something."

Marcus jerked his head back and checked the empty space behind him before returning his gaze to Ivy. "She can't have this body back. It's mine."

"You should've died that day on the freeway," Ivy countered. "That was your destiny. Instead you stole your sister's life. That makes you about the lowest life form I've ever met … and I've met some real jackoffs."

"Ivy!" Jack struggled against his restraints. "I'm going to … ."

Ivy forced herself to remain calm and focus on Marcus. Brian would be here soon. "You should run now, Marcus. This is your last chance for escape."

Marcus sneered. "Why? Are the cops coming for me? I have trouble believing that since you're here alone."

"The cops aren't coming," Ivy lied. "They think I'm crazy. I told them you took over your sister's body and now they're worried I need to be committed. In fact, they probably don't even know I'm gone yet. I climbed out my bedroom window and stole my father's car."

"Ivy," Jack whimpered. "How could you be so stupid?"

"You're brave. I'll give you that," Marcus said. "Jack is right, though. You're a moron. Why didn't you call the police and tell them where we were before coming down here? That would've been the smarter move."

"You heard Jack," Ivy replied. "I'm not known for my brains."

"You're definitely a looker," Marcus said. "I have plans for that cute little body of yours. Tell me, are you into pain?"

Ivy made a face. "You're a sick individual, Marcus," she said. "You feed off fear. Did you make your mother beg before you killed her?"

"No. I just popped her in the head twice and called it a day."

"Did you say anything to Mark Dalton before you killed him?"

"I asked him for directions to distract him," Marcus replied. "He didn't even see it coming. If it's any consolation, he was dead before he realized it. I didn't have time to play with him because I knew you and Jack were close. I couldn't have fun like I wanted."

Ivy needed a little more time, so she heaped on more questions. "Why didn't you kill me that day in the park?"

"I didn't want you dead yet," Marcus explained. "I wanted Jack to worry himself sick over you first. It worked, too. You two were miserable for days before he found his backbone – and I'm guessing another bone – and won you back. That was a little annoying because then he didn't leave your side for two days, but it worked out in the end."

"You know you could've gotten away with this if you hadn't been so bent on revenge, right?" Ivy asked.

"Jack deserves to die. He ruined my life."

"You ruined your own life," Ivy shot back, refusing to mince words. She knew a little something that Marcus didn't, and while he'd kept his attention on her she'd noticed a distant flash through the window behind him. "Do you know what your problem is, Marcus?"

"No. I have a feeling you're going to tell me, though."

"You're your own worst enemy," Ivy said, taking a step away from the bottom of the stairs to clear the way. "You never know when to take the win and shut your stupid mouth."

Marcus lunged in Ivy's direction as she covered her head and turned toward the wall. Jack's scream was anguished until he saw Brian appear out of the darkness, gun drawn. He had an army of police officers behind him.

"Laura, you're going to want to put your hands up and turn around," Brian ordered, his voice deadly. "If you put up a fight, I don't have any qualms about shooting you."

"You can't do that," Ivy whispered. "Laura needs her body back."

The look on Marcus' face was chilling. He was out of moves. If he stepped toward Jack, Brian would kill him. If he stepped toward Ivy, the outcome would be the same. There was only one victim he had left to torture.

"Well, I guess that's that," Marcus said, his eyes locking with Ivy's. "That was well played. You're smarter than you look. I take it you lied about not calling the cops."

"Jack may think I'm an idiot sometimes, but I try really hard not to live up to that reputation," Ivy shot back. "Just ... go. Let Laura back in."

"Oh, no," Marcus said, reaching behind his back and retrieving his gun. "What fun would that be?"

Multiple cops started screaming at Marcus to put down his gun ... and then they started firing. So many rounds went off Ivy lost count as she huddled close to the floor and covered her ears. When she risked a glance up a few moments later, Marcus was dead on the floor ... and so was Laura. Ivy looked around, desperate for a hint of the woman in question, but Laura was gone. Ivy had a feeling the consciousness clinging to this world passed over when Laura's body exhaled its last breath. She could only hope Laura found peace on the other side. If anyone deserved respite, it was her.

Ivy jolted when a pair of hands landed on her arm, twirling her. Jack was at her side, Brian cutting him loose before Ivy could take notice, and his face was murderous. Ivy ignored the glare and threw her arms around his neck. "I thought I lost you."

Jack rubbed her back and burst into tears, taking Ivy by surprise. "You'd better prepare yourself," he murmured, crying into her neck. "You're not going to be able to leave your bed for a week."

"I can live with that."

Twenty-Five

Ivy woke to a solid wall of muscle and Jack's arms holding her pressed tightly against his chest. She sighed, relieved that it was over and momentarily sad that Laura lost everything due to her brother's twisted mind.

"Honey, I'm still going to kill you," Jack murmured into her hair. "Before that, though, I want to hold you and then eat breakfast. We'll schedule your killing for after noon if that works for you."

Ivy snickered, pressing a soft kiss to one of Jack's scars. "Are you okay?"

"I'm fine."

Ivy wrenched her head back so she could fix Jack with a dubious look.

"Okay, I'm going to be fine," Jack corrected. "I'm a work in progress."

"You're my work in progress," Ivy said, running her finger down Jack's cheek. "Wait ... you don't want to take off now that I'm safe, do you?"

Jack growled. "No."

"That's good. I was going to have to kill *you* if that was the case."

"We're not going to be apart again," Jack said. "I've learned my lesson. This is where I want to be."

"In bed with me?" Ivy asked, her eyes twinkling.

"Every minute of every day," Jack answered. "For now I'm going to take hunkering down in this house with you for the next few days and call it a victory. We'll work on the bigger picture down the road."

"Few days? What about work?"

"I talked to Brian last night," Jack said. "Technically Bellaire is going to take the lead on this one. Marcus kidnapped me, but Mark Dalton's case is bigger. They took Laura's body into custody last night and they're handling the bulk of the paperwork.

"Brian said he would handle the stuff from our end and he told me to take the rest of the week off and spend it with you," he continued. "Since that was exactly what I wanted to do, I didn't put up much of a fight."

Ivy did the math in her head. "That means we have five whole days together."

"It does."

"I'm definitely not going to be able to walk," she mused, causing Jack to chuckle as he pressed his lips to her forehead.

"Well, as much fun as *that* is, I thought we would only spend today in bed," Jack said. "I believe you mentioned something about a hike and a picnic, and I wouldn't mind taking a drive over to Traverse City one day. How does that sound?"

"That sounds like the best offer I've had in … well … ever."

"Good," Jack said, kissing her forehead again.

"You know we're probably going to be forced into a meal with my parents, too, right? My dad was hopping mad about me stealing his car last night. I'm going to have to smooth that over."

"Yes, well, I'm going to enjoy watching him yell at you," Jack said. "Why don't we host a barbecue here? I can grill steaks for Max and me, and you can make weird vegetarian stuff for everyone else."

"Really? You want to barbecue together, too?"

"Honey, there's absolutely nothing I don't want to do with you."

"What about riding a horse?" Ivy asked.

"Except that," Jack conceded, rubbing small circles on her back as he moved his uncovered feet against hers on top of the mattress at the end of the bed.

"Can I ask you one thing before we start our day of bliss?"

"Yes."

"Do you really believe that Marcus was in Laura's body, or are you just saying it because you don't want me to feel like an idiot?" Ivy was afraid to ask the question in case Jack decided she was crazy in the light of day.

"That was definitely Marcus," Jack replied. "I don't know how he did it. I don't know how any of it happened. I don't understand how Laura came to you. I do believe it happened, though."

"What's the report going to say?"

"That Laura lost her mind and tried to avenge her brother," Jack said. "I'm sorry, honey. We'll both get locked up if we tell the other story. I … you know that, right?"

Ivy nodded. "I hope Laura found peace."

"I hope so, too," Jack said, tightening his arms around Ivy and rolling so he was on his back and she was settled on his chest. "We're going to have a fight at some point about you walking into that basement. Since I'm feeling lazy and snuggly today, I need you to pick a time later in the week."

Ivy laughed. "You want to schedule a fight?"

"Friday is good for me," Jack said. "How is it for you?"

"Do we get to make up the same night?"

"That's a must."

"Then Saturday is better for me," Ivy said. "I want to go to Traverse City on Friday."

"Deal," Jack said, kissing her softly. "Now, do you want to play here or in the kitchen first?"

Ivy rested her head on Jack's chest, listening to the soothing beat of his heart for a moment. "I want to play here first."

"That was a really good answer, honey," Jack said. "Now, let me explain the game to you … ."

"Oh, no," Ivy countered. "We're playing my game today. I'm the boss."

"Aren't you always?"

"Maybe we can share the title," Ivy suggested. "I want to be the boss first, though."

Jack pushed Ivy's mussed hair away from her face. "Okay. Just tell me when it's my turn."

"You're on."

Made in the USA
Middletown, DE
27 October 2017